S0-AVD-483

Broken Quill Society

The Mystery of Shakespeare's Bones

KIRK LAYTON

Copyright © 2017 Kirk Layton

All rights reserved.

ISBN-13:
978-1546641353

ISBN-10:
1546641351

DEDICATION

For my girls.

Chapter 1

HER CAR WAS IN THE college parking lot, and Hal threw in a suitcase, slammed the trunk shut, and took his spot in the passenger seat while holding his leather satchel.

Katherine wasn't impressed. "You've put us behind schedule." She didn't look at him, but kept her eyes on the road.

"You could've picked me up."

"I don't pick up employees."

"And I don't rush for management."

With that, they were soon on the Queen Elizabeth II highway, and Hal knew it was going to be a long, quiet ride.

He took a magazine out of his satchel. Hal subscribed to variety of academic journals and smaller literary magazines, but *Terrific Crime* was not one of them. When it had shown up in his mailbox just yesterday, he had only looked at it briefly before tossing it in the satchel for something to read when he was bored. Mind you, he did appreciate the 1950's pulp fiction drawing of a dead red-haired woman and the old-style font on the cover. Apart from that, it looked rather mundane.

"Don't even think about it." Katherine hadn't looked sideways but still knew Hal was going to adjust the seat to get comfortable. "I've got them just where I want them."

He didn't respond, but opened the magazine to the table of contents. "Katherine, get this…"

"I don't care."

"But there's an author in here with…"

"Dammit, Hal! Because of you we're so damned late I have to watch the traffic all the way to Calgary."

"…with my name."

"Don't care. Busy."

"Fine then." He'd already noticed that traffic was light and that she'd put the car on cruise control. He started reading the story, but within minutes wanted to — needed to — get out of the car.

"Katherine, any chance we could stop for a few minutes?"

"We're almost there. You should've gone before you showed up."

"It's not that. I'm just feeling a little claustrophobic."

"Now you're just being silly."

Hal put the magazine back in the satchel, realizing he couldn't read the story while Katherine sat beside him; couldn't get rid of the feeling of blood on his hands — and no matter how hard he tried — could not remember if he had written it.

*****

"TELL ME, HAL, do you often forget periods of time?"

"No. Just recently." He could feel the winter chill coming through the window of the little office on the hospital's third floor.

"And the people you talk with…you say they're from books?"

"Yes, doctor, characters from some books."

"Do they tell you what to do?"

"No. No, they just talk to me."

"Could you give me an example?"

Hal was uncomfortable with these questions. He knew what was happening wasn't normal for others, but for him it had started around age thirteen. "My favourite visit was during the summer when Walt Whitman and I hung out in the backyard. He read me some of his poetry and I read him some of mine. It was really quite civil."

"What changed to bring you here today?"

"They, my visitors, that is, used to come around every now and then, but I was always aware of the world around me. Now when they come, it's like part of the day disappears. I guess I'm here because the visits are beginning to scare me a little."

*****

"OH NO, RED DEER COLLEGE is a party school." Hal was talking to a high school student who was planning for the next stage of academia. "You have to remember that Red Deer is a smaller city so once all the students are there, then the fun begins." The student still didn't look convinced, so he gave her a brochure and she walked away.

The booth that Red Deer College had at the Calgary Stampede wasn't a booth at all. It was a portable gazebo with RDC in large bold lettering on the synthetic roof while four rather unsteady legs held it upright. It was pleasant while the sun was directly overhead, somewhat of a problem when it rained, and, as had been learned last summer, dangerous during high winds. But that, with two foldable tables, was where Hal and two student volunteers were seated.

Brandi was trying to arrange the brochures into a fan. "You know, Professor Wales, you told the last teenager that the college was, how did you put it, a 'centre for fine education'."

Hal smiled. "That last teenager had a stern-looking mother right behind him. Anyway, I'm going to take a break now. I'll be on that bench over there if anybody has a question about the college you can't answer."

Hal had been eyeing the bench in front of the college information booth for the last half-hour, waiting until it was free, which didn't happen often during the Stampede.

Once he was settled on the bench, he pulled the magazine *True Crime* out of his satchel and, once again, read "The Mystery of Shakespeare's Bones."

He used the whetstone and slid it along the blade of his favourite sword in a slow, rhythmic motion. For Hal Wales, this was a time for contemplation of all the planning he had done over several months. When Katherine had been invited to give the keynote presentation at a conference, Hal had realized the story he had heard long before was real. He had travelled to England on his own last summer, claiming he was researching another book, and had prepared a trap. And now the trip was booked, the location where he could hold her was secured. Soon he would have millions of dollars.

He held the sword hilt with both hands and sliced the air. "It's too bad I can't take this with me, but it'll never get through security at the airport. I guess the one I hid in Oxford will have to suffice. Just a few days and it'll all be over."

He checked the time and ate a quick breakfast of toast with orange marmalade before riding the city bus to his job at Red Deer College. As he walked to his office, he could see the woman he worked for, the one he wanted to kill, waiting impatiently for him to arrive.

"Good morning, Dr. Minola," he said.

"You're late," she said, trying not to notice the way he was looking at her. She didn't want to think it, but she had worn an extra tight blouse today, knowing they had a meeting.

"Sorry, but the bus was late again," he said.

Hal looked around, expecting someone to be noticing his discomfort with the details in the story. Seeing no one watching him, he flipped a couple of pages and continued reading

"What do I do now?" she thought. Katherine was looking for help from someone she sometimes found to be intimidating when he argued with her. She sometimes said that if anything happened to her, the police should be told to treat Hal as a suspect.

He said, "It's alright, Katherine. We'll find who put that threatening note under your hotel room door. Why don't you sit on my bed and tell me all about your research. I've always wanted to know about it."

He had always been jealous of Katherine's success, but before he could do anything to her, he needed to find out where the iron chest was hidden.

"But I don't want to tell you, Hal," she said. She sat closer. Maybe she was wrong about him.

He said, "It is hard to help you if I don't know the secret that other people want to know." Hal held her close.

"Oh, Hal! I'm so happy you're looking at me like that. I always thought you didn't like me. Make love to me!" she said enthusiastically.

Hal knew there was something wrong with sitting on a public bench reading a story that was devolving into poorly written erotica with people walking around him. He turned several pages, skipping that section.

The room in the basement was dark because the single 40-watt bulb didn't give off very much light. The concrete walls oozed a kind of thick, black water that even made the rats nervous. The tension in the air was thick, and Hal knew why. He almost had his answer.

Katherine was tied to a chair with ropes taken from an old tool chest Hal had found while scouting out this area. There were many old buildings in Oxford, but this one had seemed to him to be older than the rest, which was why he had chosen it. There was something symbolic in this because he knew that what he was looking for was many, many years old. He cut off some of her long red hair to keep as a souvenir and took the time to tie it together into a little knot he could keep in his pocket.

"I know the iron chest is hidden around here, so tell me exactly where," he whispered to Katherine. He knew he was only moments away from getting the answer he wanted. "Tell me where the bones of Shakespeare are hidden," he said.

"No, I will never tell you!" she yelled. She had spent too much time gathering the information that could make her famous, and she didn't want to share it. Besides, he couldn't hurt her now that they were lovers, could he?

"Then you will leave me little choice but to hurt your family," he grinned heinously. "They'll never see me coming because I'll stay in the shadows. I'll track each one down and hurt them if you don't tell me the location of the treasure. I know you found it. That's why I won't let you go to the conference and tell everyone. The treasure is mine and only mine."

"No, please," said Katherine, sobbing. "Don't hurt them. I'll tell you everything if you don't hurt them and let me go."

He listened to her explain where he would find the treasure, making sure he had all the details he need. Satisfied, Hal picked up his sword. He placed it on the rope as if to cut it. He said, "I told you I would let you go. I lied." He pushed and watched the sword blade go into her body.

"Only I can have the treasure, and I won't tell anyone, even the readers of my story, where it is. Find me if you can."

His hands were numb as he held the magazine. Turning back to the first page of the story, he rubbed his finger on his name under the title. As poorly as the story was written, some of it was true. In one of the satchel's pockets were his passport and the agenda Katherine had had him make for the conference in Oxford they were going to that afternoon.

*****

"YOU KNOW, I DON'T believe everything you're telling me."

"Why would I lie to you? I'm the one who checked in for observation. This is all voluntary, you know?"

"I understand that, Hal, but as your doctor for the next couple of weeks, I need to know everything. I'm just not buying the story that cutesy characters come to talk to you and that sometimes time disappears. Try again."

Hal put his head into his hands and rubbed his face before speaking. "When I was younger, it was like that. Now, well, now it's like a rush of sound. It's kind of like music made of voices, but I can't hear just a single one, and a darkness that really isn't darkness but a movement where you can't see what is moving." He looked up. "This isn't making any sense, is it?"

"Yes, it actually does. It started when you hit puberty. What was happening in your life when it got worse?"

"I started looking for my mother."

*****

"EXCUSE ME, but are you Professor Wales?

"Yes, that's me." Hal refocused his thoughts and looked up at the middle-aged woman standing in front of him.

"You don't look much like a professor to me, if you don't mind me saying that, of course."

Hal stood up as he didn't feel like inviting her to sit beside him. "How can I help you today?"

"I was just talking with the students at the college information booth, and they said you could answer some questions. Seriously, you look like you're still in high school. Have you finished any degrees?"

"I'm 27 and, yes, I have a doctorate in literature."

"Well, that means you certainly can't have much experience teaching. How do I make sure my son gets more experienced teachers? He's very talented, and I don't want him taught by just anyone."

This was nothing Hal hadn't heard before. Still, he smiled and waited until she finished. "You can check the profile pages on the English department website. It lists everyone's qualifications. However, you need to realize that if your son wants to succeed, he'll have to get through one of my classes."

"Perhaps I'll consider other schools for him, then." She quickly turned and left before Hal could respond.

He put his right foot on the bench and re-tied the sneaker's shoelace. The phone in his satchel had already beeped twice to remind him of a meeting and he went back to the information booth.

"It's such a wonderful day, but I'm afraid I have to go. I promise I'll bring you back some rock candy from England. Oh, and somebody else will be along shortly to help out."

One of the students motioned to the side and walked from the booth to talk out of earshot of anyone else. "Hal. I mean, I can call you Hal, right."

"Well, Brandi, we're not in a classroom, so I guess that's fine."

"I just wanted to thank you for that grade you gave me and all the extra help passing the class."

"You're welcome, but I was just doing my job, and you earned the mark."

"Really, though, I'm speaking for a bunch of us in the class. We kinda thought you might like a little bit of fun stuff." She looked around to make sure nobody was watching before taking a little pill bottle out of her pocket. "We call them berries. It's kinda new and if you wanna have a fun time…"

"No."

"Look, we just wanna help you out a little."

"Look, this is wrong on too many levels. You could be arrested in a second, kicked out of college…"

"And what could happen to you if everyone knew?"

"Knew what?"

"Where you spent Christmas vacation. We know things, and we can teach you a couple of things. Just take the berries."

"Yes, I'm sure we could teach each other a couple of things. But I do need to go kill Katherine. Meet, I mean meet Katherine."

Chapter 2

TRYING, OR NOT TRYING — to find a handful of people in the crowds attending the Calgary Stampede requires advance planning. Hal knew where the department meeting was; what he wanted was the slowest route to get there. Being late was easily accomplished as there's no such thing as a straight line when you walk through a midway. He was halfway to his destination when he noticed a problem at one of the games.

"Could I help?"

The young woman he asked was in charge of three children who were all strapped into chairs. She pointed to the smallest girl. "She wants to play but can't, and I'm trying to figure out why this one is crying. Anything you can do would be appreciated."

Hal stooped beside the child. "Would you like me to throw some rings for you?" He saw a slight nod of the head and a smile.

Hal got the attention of the carnie operating the game. "Hey, buddy, how many tries for a toonie?"

"Two bucks gets six tries. You only have to ring three and get your pick from the toys on the bottom row here."

"You mean those little things? I can't even tell what they are."

"Right you are. All you have to do is get the rings around the necks of three soda pop bottles. It's just that easy. And if you ring all six, you win a little bear."

"And how would I get the big bear you have front and centre? You know, the one surrounded by the signs that say *Win this bear.*"

"All you need to do is trade in three of the little bears. Don't worry, it's a fair game and the kids win bears all day long."

Hal bent down. "I'm going to try and win you a prize. The trick is to aim for the closest ones to you." He began to throw, aiming with care.

"Hey, fella, you got two on, so you're learning fast." The carnie was talking loudly, hoping to attract more attention to what many thought of as an out-of-date game. "Don't let an easy game beat you, though. What-da-ya-say?"

"Another try it is." Hal looked down at the girl "This time I'm going to aim for the middle ones and see what happens."

"Oh, so close, but only two on again." The carnie had increased his volume even more as others had approached the game to watch and play. "Impress the ladies and win them a bear. All the ladies love bears."

"It's not for the ladies. It's for this little girl here who can't play herself so give me one more chance." Hal watched as the carnie ran around the game to give a prize to another competitor before taking his money and handing him more rings. Grinning at the child, he told her "Sometimes it's best not to overthink things. Just take everything you're trying to do, wind up and let her rip." He threw the handful of rings into the air without trying to aim.

"Three, the gentleman here ringed three." The carnie was more than happy to give away a little prize as the group around his game had grown even larger with people waiting for their turn to play. "Here's your prize for ringing three. Hey, how about another go? Come on, you know this is a kid's game? How many would like to see our skinny friend go one more time and show everyone what an adult can do at a kid's game."

Hal waved the carnie away and bent down to give the prize to the little girl.

"Hey, what're doing there? Get away from her!" The speaker was a rather large and very angry man.

"Sorry, but her assistant said I could play the game for her because she can't."

"What assistant? I'm her father and I think you need to take a couple steps back."

Hal realized all the children had fathers standing beside their chairs, and none of the men looked happy. "No, really, there was someone here. There's been a misunderstanding, I'm sure, so I'll leave."

"That would be a good idea."

Hal walked away in a slight state of confusion, no longer sure if somebody had asked him for help. He looked at his prize: an American July 4th ring.

He slipped the ring into his leather satchel. As he did so, he saw something else next to the crime magazine. When he had played the game for the child, he kept the satchel at his feet, so it didn't make sense that there was now a small knot of red hair inside it. He threw the hair into a garbage can, realizing his hands were slightly shaking. There was a root beer stand nearby, and Hal used a small soda to wash down a little white pill from the bottle in his satchel. He leaned against a security fence until his hands stopped shaking, before continuing on his way to find the meeting.

"There they are." The rest of the English department faculty were at a pair of picnic tables and Hal sat down at the end of one of them.

Katherine already had the meeting underway. "Although it may sound silly, we're being asked to mark assignments using blue or black ink as red is a negative colour for students even at the college level. Hal, how nice of you to join us. Do you have any thoughts on this?"

He didn't say anything, but he looked at her red hair for a few moments.

"If you don't have anything valuable to add, then we'll move on. There've been concerns expressed from the college president's office about inappropriate behaviour amongst some faculty where students are concerned. I was told to remind everybody that if you start a romantic relationship with a student, you must fill out a form and let me know, especially if that person is currently taking a class with you. Unfortunately, there's already been an incident of a certain female student spending time with a math lecturer in exchange for a better grade. And no, for those men here, I won't tell you who she is. Let's just say the lecturer in question could be out of a job before September rolls around, which I don't see as being entirely fair. So, I made sure that student won't graduate when she was planning to. Now, are there any questions? Yes, April, what is it?"

"I really think that if I taught an advanced class once in a while, I'd be able to show you how talented I am." Hal knew the speaker had been hired a year before to teach Children's Literature, but he couldn't remember her last name. "I mean, I like teaching the introductory classes, but I want to teach senior classes."

"That won't happen until you have more experience." Katherine's back had straightened as it always did when dealing with a troublesome student, or, for that matter, a member of the college faculty.

"Look, Kate, all I'm asking for is to be given a chance at teaching some of those senior level courses, just like everyone else."

"The name is Dr. Minola," Katherine's voice had taken on a slight edge. "And you will treat me with the respect my position as Chair of the Department of English deserves. You need more publications before teaching other classes. Hal, Hal … do you ever listen? What was your last book called? *Follow Trains?*"

"Not exactly, it was called *Follow the Line: The Importance of Rail Travel on Canadian Fiction.*"

"Right, and the one before that was *Follow the Atwood Legacy.* Always following something, right Hal? Never leading?"

She looked back at a red-faced young woman. "So, anyway, more publications and, I suspect, more experience teaching at other institutions will lead to teaching higher level classes." Katherine pursed her lips and gave a slight nod to indicate that the discussion was finished. "As for the rest of you, over the next few days you'll be expected to work at the information booth alongside several of our top students, promoting the college to all high school students and their parents. Further, as you know I'll be heading to England in a few hours to present the keynote address on William Shakespeare at the Oxford Bodleian library this Saturday. Make sure you email Hal if there're any concerns. Hal, can you tell you them where I'll be if they need to get in touch with me?"

"Somehow, Katherine, I don't suspect that'll be much of a problem."

Katherine ignored him and went back to informing everyone how she expected all of them to have their fall class syllabi ready for approval by the time the summer was over. Hal was already bored with her constant talking and began to look at the movement of the crowd. If he relaxed his eyes a little, he could see a pattern emerging in the chaos. There was a regular flow coming from a large tent to the right where a television news team did live reports. Those people had to walk through a line waiting to get into an open-air beer patio, which was already full. As a result, those in a hurry shoved through the line as if on a mission to destroy anything in their path. That would mean someone who was a little drunk would go off course. He pushed a stroller containing a child out of harm's way before a drunken oil executive in a cowboy outfit stumbled into that spot, careened, and left without an apology. Katherine used her fingertips to daintily push it back.

The meeting ended with most people leaving quickly and April staying to talk to Katherine privately. Hal and George were left sitting at the table.

"You know, what that woman needs is a good screwing."

"George, come on." This wasn't the kind of conversation Hal wanted to have. "So, when's your time to volunteer at the information booth?"

"I'm not on until late tonight when the drunken cowgirls always come around. I still don't understand why you agreed to go to England with her. Mind you, I bet she could be fun if her mouth was shut. She's not that much older than you, and you're even the same height. You two make a cute couple walking together on campus."

"Knock it off. There's something I need to do over there anyway."

"Mind me asking?"

"No — you see — I have another idea where to look for information about my mother."

"I remember you talking about that just before Christmas. Do you know anything more about her this time?"

"No, but I may have an idea where I was born, at least. I'm actually meeting with someone in a few minutes who may have some more information."

"Does Katherine know you're doing this when you're supposed to be helping her?"

"She doesn't need to know anything about my private life."

"I agree. It's none of her business."

"What's none of my business?" Katherine had walked over after ending her conversation with April.

"Oh, nothing much." George waved his hand in a dismissive fashion. "Did you settle things with April?"

"She made a comment about how it wasn't finished and ran away. I don't suppose either of you want to teach Children's Literature? No? I didn't think so. George, you'll need to take her shifts at the college booth, so you better get over there now."

"Well, that doesn't seem quite fair. Maybe I'll stop by the beer tent on the way there."

"I don't want beer on your breath while you're in the booth, so wait until after to meet your cowgirl friends."

George was already on his way with, as Hal thought, the slow walk of someone who had spent most of his youth on the back of a horse. In reality, it was the walk of someone who was close to retirement and didn't have any reason to hurry.

"Look at him." Katherine pointed at George. "He's in the cowboy spirit with boots and a hat. Even I wore blue jeans and a checkered shirt and I'm not working at the booth. So what's your deal showing up in a tee-shirt and sneakers?"

"This is what I always wear."

"I asked everyone to dress western."

"I'm also wearing blue jeans."

"Which look like they were painted on."

"Thanks for noticing."

"Enough of that. I always treat the lecturer who gets the best student evaluations to a reward and this year it's you. What would you like? And keep in mind we have to get our flight soon."

"Katherine, there's something I need to do first. Can I catch up with you somewhere?"

"What now?" She tapped her watch. "Time, we have limited time, remember."

"It won't take that long."

"Meet me in the casino at the blackjack tables in twenty minutes max. I could use a little more spending money."

Hal immediately turned to the right and began walking quickly. There's a section of the midway with rides for pre-schoolers and he had been expected there ten minutes ago. The woman he met was trying to corral two young children, but, seeing him, signalled to an older woman who immediately took them to another ride.

"Sorry, I'm a little late."

"Not to worry, Hal. My kids are having fun and so is their grandma." The woman speaking looked like the classic downtown office worker from some oil company who had dressed up for the Stampede. The hair under the cowboy hat was styled, her smile revealed perfect white teeth, and even her cowboy boots looked like they were by a top-end designer. Nobody would guess that she made a living snapping pictures of cheating husbands, finding debtors, or in this case, tracking down lost documents. Her business card simply read *Michelle Hammar, Gumshoe*.

"You said you have something to show me?"

"This took some time to find. When a mistake is made, there's a reason to keep it hidden." She handed Hal a brown envelope and waited until he had removed the two pages inside. "This is part of the police report."

Hal scanned the first document. It consisted of a form with spaces filled in showing a date and location but nothing of significance. "This is rather difficult to read."

"Whoever filled it in used pencil instead of pen and then the whole thing has been photocopied a couple of times."

It was the second page that caught Hal off guard. Near the top, barely legible, was his name, but spread out in way that was difficult to process. He held it up to the light as his brain began to realize that the pencilled writing had been smudged. As it was a photocopy, holding it up didn't help, but he did begin to see the words that had been smudged some 27 years earlier. He read them out loud. "Baby boy — about 3 months — found in hallway at Prince of Wales Hotel." He looked at Michelle. "Hallway Wales. My name isn't Hal Wales. It's where I was found."

Michelle waited until Hal's breathing became regular again before speaking. "Near the bottom of the page, it says that social services recommended you be placed into foster care until your parents could be found. Problem is, Hal, I can't find anything that says anyone looked. They put you in the system and forgot about it."

"But how did that become my name?"

"I'm thinking somebody at the hospital tried to make out what it said. If you look here," she pointed at the form, "they put it all in the section where a name goes. A nurse may have thought that would do until it was corrected."

"England, then?"

"Like I told you last time, Hal, I think the next step is to check in England."

Hal nodded and left, processing this new information while trying not to scream.

*****

KATHERINE NOTICED HAL when he walked into the blackjack room, so she scooped up her new chips and exchanged them for cash at the teller. "Well, where would you like to go?"

Hal started to count possibilities on his fingers. "We could go to the beer tent ourselves, sample everything they're selling on the midway that's deep fried, maybe stay at the casino and pretend we can count cards..." With each idea, Katherine shook her head no. "Fine then, what do you think I should want to do?"

Katherine gave a coy smile as she did have something in mind. "Hal, you like mysteries. Want to go see the yellow house?"

"The place where they found those skeletons? Sure. It's nearby, isn't it?"

"A five-minute walk at best."

"Let's go."

When the Stampede grounds were built, the surrounding neighbourhood had been still rather upscale. Time and circumstances had not been kind to the area, although there were signs of improvements. Many of the rundown houses were already replaced by modern in-fills, which allowed two houses on a lot once occupied by a single home. The owners of these new homes had little tolerance for crime and had started a Block Watch program that forced working girls and their clients to other parts of the city. The residents had long wanted the yellow house torn down, and because of recent events they were getting their way.

Most of the tourists walking past the house on their way to the Stampede grounds didn't know the history of the old building. All they saw was another house being prepared for demolition. In spite of the crowds on the sidewalks, Hal and Katherine were there in less than ten minutes.

"That's one ugly shade of yellow. How long ago was it painted like that, Katherine?"

"It's been yellow for as long as anyone can remember."

"When was it built?"

"You and your questions. I think around 1900 or so, but what do I look like, a real estate agent?"

"Just asking. It must have been one of the first houses in the area, I guess."

"Want to go inside?"

"Come on, Katherine, there's a policeman right there."

"No, that's a security guard. The police finished here, but the owners got tired of people breaking in, so it's being watched until it's torn down. I gave him a few bucks last week and he let me in."

The guard tipped his hat to them. He was busy renting spaces in the yard to people wanting to park near the Stampede.

"I love that front door, Katherine. Look at the flowers in the stained glass window. I hope they don't junk everything."

"I hear that a couple of T.V. shows want to film here. One wants psychics to ask the dead for answers, and the other one wants to check for valuables like that stained glass. Let's hit the basement."

"Man, they ripped this place apart." Hal used his phone to take a picture. The walls had been torn down and much of the cement basement floor had been broken, with the ground underneath dug into. "Is this where the skeletons were found?"

"Right in those strange looking holes where the walls used to be. They were digging up part of the basement to try to cap a sewer line before ripping the house down, and surprise: five decomposed bodies in the wall."

"The wall? Not the floor?"

"Nope. They say it looks like he took part of the foundation down and then dug into the wall to bury them."

"You'd think after five men went missing, someone would've started looking."

"But remember that was a long time ago, and they didn't go missing all at once. They figure it was done over a few years because they weren't all in the same spot, and the way they were buried was a little different each time."

"Sounds like he was getting better with practice."

"There's an unsettling thought."

"So, they know who did it then?"

"Don't you bother reading the newspaper with breakfast?"

"Oh, right. I didn't pay that much attention what with all the finals I was trying to mark. I do remember hearing something about a boy who wound up dead in a bar fight."

"The owner's son. Just after he was kicked out of the University of Toronto. Smart kid, but probably a psychopath. That wasn't the first school he got into, but his behaviour was strange so even the money his daddy had couldn't keep him in school for long."

"Man, this is the real thing then. You never get to see something like this. Can I see his room?"

"Well, I think the newspaper said it's on the top floor overlooking the street."

They made their way upstairs, avoiding chunks of concrete and a stair banister that was slightly leaning.

"This is disappointing." The room was small, empty, and damp. Stains on the wall showed that the roof leaked badly.

"You need to remember that after he was killed, his parents sort of gave up and lost the family fortune. It got converted into a rooming house at some point." Katherine had already seen the room and looked out the window while she spoke.

Hal only heard half of what was said. He imagined what the room would have originally looked like. He could see the young man in his baggy pants with greased hair and a flapper girlfriend. His room would have been full of books and playbills for whatever theatre group was coming to the city. "That closet there. I bet that's what he used."

"The police went all over the house looking for anything."

Hal ran his hands over the interior of the closet. "You're right. It's been renovated. But it's not square."

"What do you mean?"

"Check it out. The closet's wider than the door, which is often normal. But this one side isn't as big as the other. Builders wouldn't have made it that way. Find me something heavy."

Katherine returned momentarily with a spindle from the banister. "Try this."

"Listen. If I tap the wall right here it doesn't sound right. Well, they're tearing the place down anyway, so I don't think anybody will mind." He swung the spindle and put a hole in the wall. "I'm glad it's lath and plaster. This is easy to take apart."

"What've you got there?"

"It's a false wall. But it's only a couple inches in front of another wall. Oh wait. It's in front of a chimney. Maybe they built it this way after all. Oh well, I started so I may as well rip out some more."

"What's that, Hal? Down there by the mop board. When you hit the wall, it made a straight crack in the paint."

"Look at that. It's a little panel at the bottom of the wall. I bet someone painted over it and didn't even notice. It made a little secret storage place like they'd have used for valuables."

"Is there something in it? Gold maybe?"

"Yes, but not gold. A book? It's a little book alright."

Katherine took it and opened it. "Interesting. It's a surprise it didn't turn to mould back there."

"The heat from the chimney must've kept it dry. Is it a diary or something like that? That'd be spooky."

"Nope. Check it out." She gave it back to Hal.

"What is it? Are you kidding me? That guy killed and buried bodies here and we find this in his secret compartment."

"Well, I guess he really was a good student after all."

"But why hide a copy of Shakespeare, Katherine? This wouldn't have been worth that much even back then."

"Is anything written in it?"

"There's a few underlined passages, but that's all. I guess we should turn this over to the police."

"Why bother? That won't help them figure anything out. Just keep it."

"It might be wrong, but what the heck." He placed it into his satchel beside *Terrific Crime*.

"Is there anything else in there?" Katherine asked.

Hal peered in the hole. "I think there is." He used the spindle to take a larger section of the closet wall down. "It's up against the chimney, but I think I can get it out."

"Good Lord, that's a sword."

"Katherine, do you know how those people were killed?"

She looked for information with her phone while Hal gave the sword a careful inspection.

"It says here," Katherine scrolled through a couple pages, "that the evidence leans to a long knife of some sort. And what you're holding sure fits that description."

"It's called a short sword. It's got the classic look with a wide steel blade and a brass hilt."

"You know about swords?"

"We've worked together for two years, and you've never asked about my private life. Yes, I know a little bit about swords. Look at these hallmarks near the hilt."

"What do they tell you?"

"It was made in France around 1890. If this is what was used, we need to get it to the police."

"First, let's see if anything else was missed."

"I take it you're feeling a little adventuresome, Katherine."

"No. I just hate incompetence. That sword should've been found when the house was searched."

Hal set the sword down as they began to inspect the other rooms, taking great pains to look in closets and cupboards for anything overlooked by the police. Little was found besides a couple of teacups and a mouse nest. They were in a back room on the main floor when they heard the sound of someone descending the stairs from the second level. Katherine was the first to see what had happened.

"Son of a bitch! Hal, he took the sword!"

They followed a middle-aged man wearing blue jeans and a red checkered shirt outside where Katherine yelled to the security guard. "Hey! He stole a sword from the house!"

The crowded street made it difficult to hurry as both sidewalks and the roads were packed with those heading to and from the Stampede. The guard, however, made up ground and within three blocks had tackled the thief.

By the time Hal and Katherine caught up, the thief was sitting next to a parked car while the guard was talking to the police.

It was Katherine who spoke first. "Well, here's the jackass. What were you going to do, sell the sword online?"

"Bugger off."

"Now there's a fascinating reply. No matter. You'll be in jail soon."

"And you'll be dead soon anyway."

"What the hell did you just say?"

"Ask him." The thief nodded in Hal's direction before springing to his feet and shoving the guard out of the way. His movement was enough of a surprise that the others didn't react quickly enough. They were well behind the thief when he ducked under a barrier that had lowered over the road. Everyone who noticed yelled at the same time, but the thief, believing he had found a sure way to escape, didn't heed the warnings.

In Calgary, the barriers lower when a sensor tells of an oncoming train. Hal turned away while Katherine tried to follow where the body landed.

"What the…we need to talk to the police."

"We can't miss our flight."

"Katherine, he's dead. He was running from us."

"No, he was a thief and he was just running. That's in a not my problem category."

"But still…"

The guard took both of them by the shoulders. "Guys, you have to do me a favour here."

"A favour?" Hal was confused. "What do you mean, a favour?"

"Well, I'm going to be in shit for letting him get away and for letting him get into the house to start with so…"

"So what?"

"Don't be so dense Hal." Katherine had caught the guard's implication. "He's trying to save his job. He let the thief get away; he sold parking spots on the lawn. If they find out he let us in on top of that then he's fired for sure."

The guard nodded.

"Let's go, Hal. This is a waste of time. I just hope the sword wasn't damaged."

Ha; stood for few moments with a perplexed look before giving up. They walked back to Katherine's car at the Stampede parking lot.

"There's just one thing I need to know, Hal." She unlocked the car doors. "What did that guy mean by me being dead soon?"

Hal gripped the satchel a little tighter. It would be easy to tell her and let her read the story. "Honestly Katherine, I have no idea."

"He said to ask you."

He buckled his seat belt and helped look for a clear route out of the parking lot. They were on the freeway before Katherine asked again. "What did that thief mean about asking you about my being dead?"

"Give it a rest, Katherine. I don't know anything."

She didn't hear him as she quickly had other issues to deal with. The freeway had become quite congested.

"Hal, watch the lane on your side for me. I swear, every time I drive on this road, people try to get me. Look at this guy ahead of me. Hey buddy! Try the other pedal; it makes the car go faster! Where'd you get your licence, a box of Cracker Jacks!"

"You know, Katherine, Deerfoot Trail does have more than one lane. In fact, that one to the left is the fast lane where people who want to drive over the speed limit are often found."

"The last thing I need right now is you being the classic backseat driver. But you want me in the fast lane? Alright, now we're in the fast lane."

"You didn't shoulder check."

"I didn't have time."

"You didn't drive this way this morning."

"I didn't have a flight to catch, did I! Why don't you have a licence by the way? Then you could drive yourself and stop telling me how to."

"Fine. Just watch for other cars."

"Now who is this idiot on my bumper?"

Hal could make out the car in the side view mirror and realized it was indeed far too close. Only the week prior, there had been a multi-car pileup on the freeway which had sent several people to the hospital, and he didn't want to be another statistic. "Maybe we should just get into the centre lane again."

"I would like to, but take a look."

He turned to the right and saw the line of semis blocking any chance of changing lanes. "Well, they should all be in the far right lane that's meant for big trucks. This doesn't seem right at all."

"Doesn't seem right? That's quite the comment. Hal check out how close this guy is getting now."

He managed to look behind him to the left as a large white sedan came up on their bumper. "He's way too close."

"Stay focused. Just stay focused." Katherine wasn't talking to Hal but to herself. There was a pickup truck in front that, while speeding, was still not going quickly enough for her to accelerate and outrun the sedan behind her. For her part, Katherine kept her focus and didn't allow her car to move out of its lane. "Damn this guy! He backs off a little and then speeds up like he's going to run into me. He's done it three times."

With the semis to her left out of the way, she merged over to the centre lane. The sedan rolled up alongside, and they both watched as the driver tipped his hat before disappearing up the freeway.

Hal tried to loosen the seatbelt to breathe easier. "Well, if you're feeling like it, I guess we could just finish going to the airport instead of calling the police. I couldn't make out his licence plate. It was all covered with mud."

Katherine didn't want to say that at that moment she wouldn't have been able to release her grip from the steering wheel even if she did stop. "At least he tipped his hat at me."

"I thought he was covering his face."

"Hal, do you think he wanted to…I mean there was no reason to…did he want to run us off the road?"

"Oh, I'm sure it was nothing like that. Maybe it was someone late for a flight."

"I don't believe that. Not for a minute."

Hal rubbed both temples this time. He didn't believe it either.

Chapter 3

"OH, HERE WE GO." The seatbelt sign came on and the standard announcement was made asking people to return to their seats and put on their seatbelts as the plane began to shake. Hal tightened his even though it was already snug.

"Feeling nervous, are you? You know the centre seat is far safer." The middle-aged woman hadn't introduced herself when Hal sat down. She had, however, complained loudly when she realized that, because she hadn't booked her seat in advance, she would have to sit in the middle of the row. "All we need to do is switch seats and you'll feel much better."

"I think it would be best if I sat here just in case I have to, you know, throw up a little." She tried to signal the flight attendant to request being moved again while Hal kept a straight face.

He knew it was rude, but he started listening in on the conversations around him as a distraction from the shaking plane. There was the young couple from Meadow Lake, Saskatchewan, on their first international vacation talking about how much they hoped to meet someone from the royal family. There was the aging hockey player who had recently been released from the Edmonton Oilers telling his rather bored seatmate his entire life story.

The plane seemed to sink a few feet and even the flight attendants looked at each other in concern before putting on their standard everything is just fine smile.

If he listened closely he could hear the Scottish school teacher who was explaining to a seatmate how Victoria, British Columbia, looked more like London than London does. "I tell you, if I could get a teaching job in Victoria, I'd never go back to Dennyloadhead. The little rotters I have to teach are going to be the death of me. You'd think that by the time they turned seven, they'd know how to get to the toilet on time."

Half way through the flight, Hal noticed the flight attendants had sat down and tightened their seatbelts.

"Hello from the flight deck. This is your co-pilot, Jeremy, and I just wanted to explain the rough ride. We've hit a storm over the Arctic but it will only last for a little longer and then it should be clear sailing from there to London. We ask that you stay in your seats at this time, and I'm afraid that meal services will be delayed until we're out of the storm." Hal smiled as people cheered when they heard they wouldn't have to eat airline food for a little longer.

Hal had done his best to alleviate the stress of airline travel in advance by making sure he was in a seat on the aisle and that he was seven rows back from the curtain between coach and first class. The aisle seat meant that he couldn't see out the plane's windows, and the seventh row meant when the service trolley went by, he had a clear shot to the plane's centre bathrooms while others had to wait for the trolley to pass. The turbulence was something he couldn't anticipate.

The plane banked slightly to the left and then made a sudden move to the right. Hal looked at the woman next to him and found she was fast asleep thanks to a couple over-the-counter muscle relaxers and a mini bottle of Jack Daniels.

"And then Katherine gets it." It was all Hal heard over the noise, but it was enough. He strained to hear more, but his efforts were unsuccessful, and with the noise he doubted he had heard anything. Yet, all he could think was that someone was talking about his Katherine and that meant somebody else knew what was going on.

With the stretch of bad weather behind them, the meal service began and was quickly cleared away. The overhead cabin lights were turned off, and people stopped talking and plugged into the entertainment system to watch severely edited movies. Hal took out his satchel, which had been stored under the seat in front of him as per the directions — or was it an order — of the male attendant. In it were the forms he wanted to review one last time. They had the letterhead of a hospital and once empty spaces that had been filled in with as much information as possible. Once again, he checked names and dates to ensure that there were no mistakes on his part.

"Excuse me."

Hal looked up at an attendant. "Hmmm?"

"There's a lady up in first class who wanted me to bring this back to you."

Hal lowered his tray and a single cookie on a napkin was placed in front of him.

"I take it you know the woman who sent this?"

"Yes, she's my supervisor at work."

"So, she gets to sit up front and you're stuck back here? Well, isn't it just so special that she sent you a cookie."

"It's more than she normally does."

"Perhaps I'll turn up the air conditioning a bit more. She's using a blanket to keep warm."

"Chunky chocolate chip. At least she knows the kind I like; that almost makes up for sitting back here."

"Cookies? We get cookies?" The woman beside Hal was stirring.

The attendant just smiled. "I'm sorry, dear, but not everyone gets cookies." He left before a string of profanities were directed his way.

With the cookie finished, Hal made his way to the washroom seven rows away and then turned and walked to the one in the back of the plane. On the way, he looked for someone he knew or just someone who would have used the name Katherine in a conversation. The problem was that he couldn't hear anything. He closed his eyes and tried harder, but there was no way to hear anything, even a few feet away, over the noise of a plane. "What did I hear then?" The conversations…from other trips…other planes…conversations they had…with me. Then there is no one…"

"Hey buddy, would you move it? You're blocking the aisle standing there talking to yourself."

Hal hurried back and picked up an envelope someone had left on his seat. It was normal for Katherine to leave notes and tasks on Hal's desk when he wasn't around so, without thinking, he placed it in the seat pocket. He used a foot to retrieve his satchel and take out the Shakespeare book from the yellow house.

The book focused on the *Henry IV* and *Henry V* plays. Hal thumbed through the edition carefully to make sure he didn't damage any of the aged pages. Because he was careful, he began to notice a pattern. Some of the lines in the plays had been underlined with pencil. Most of the marks were so light he could hardly see them.

There was a different section that caught Hal by surprise. The section in *Henry V* where the boys were killed behind the battle lines had been underlined so many times the pencil had almost gone through the page. So had the famous soliloquy about sending men into the breach. Hal forgot where he was and spoke out loud. "I wonder if that's why he buried men in the wall?"

"What was that?" The woman beside him wasn't looking impressed.

"Sorry. Nothing. I was just talking to myself."

"Well, stop it. You woke me up again. And do you really need that light on?"

"Yes. I'm doing some reading."

"Well, do it quietly; I'm trying to sleep."

He returned to the book, checking it from front to back for anything else that had been underlined. There wasn't even an owner's name on the first page. Hal flipped to the empty back pages and found something else so faint he was forced to hold it to the light. He found a couple names under the heading of Toronto, one under Ottawa, and five names under Calgary. Holding the page to the light once again, he found pencilling that was so faded he thought he was reading an indentation: The Breach.

He wanted to tell someone, but didn't know how to say it. *Hi, you don't know me but I know who did a whole bunch of murders. Oh, and I watched a guy get killed by a train today. That reminds me, I might kill a woman in first class.* The pain in his temples was increasing and he closed his eyes, trying to make the day end without yelling.

*****

"YOU NEED TO learn how to do some breathing exercises. This will help calm you when you're under stress."

"Doctor, you told me there were plenty of medications that could act quickly." Hal didn't want the doctor to know, but he had had an episode half way through the night. He had seen a darkness flow through a closed window, circle the bed he lay in, and revolve endlessly before it collapsed on him. When he woke, he was standing beside the door with his hand on the knob, certain that something bad was happening on the other side. What he didn't want was to be put on a 24-hour watch, so he kept it to himself. "Just a little something to take the edge off, maybe."

"Many of them could result in a dependency, and you don't want that to happen, trust me. Learn how to control your breathing, slow down your heart, and you might even find that you can make yourself drift off to a nap. So don't do it while you're driving."

"I don't drive."

"Right, too many things happening at once and you can't focus on them. Let's try the first exercise, shall we?"

*****

IT WAS AN HOUR later that a crying child woke him and, looking for a new way to pass the time, Hal took the envelope that had been left on his seat from the seat pocket he had stashed it in. He didn't know what to expect as Katherine had time to talk to him before the plane left Calgary so leaving him a file didn't make sense. There were only three pages in the envelope, but each page consisted of several photographs. He studied each page and each individual photograph carefully. Some of the photos were at least a year old and were fairly generic: either himself or Katherine alone, and a few together at various college events ranging from theatrical performance to school sports. There were others that had been taken only a few hours ago at the Stampede and going into the yellow house. It was the third page that was the most disturbing. In a red fine marker were the words *kill her*. The photos had been taken with a long-range camera and showed Katherine in various stages of undress. Hal placed them back in the envelope and then put the envelope in his satchel. He was beginning to get a feeling of darkness circling the plane and the sounds of someone dying in his ears. There was no choice but to swallow another pill, as breathing exercises would not be enough this time.

Chapter 4

"HAL, WOULD YOU stop lollygagging."

"I'll be there in a minute." Hal was once again trying to look at the other passengers as one of them had to be involved with this strange plot. It wasn't until they boarded the Gatwick Express to downtown London that they sat together at a small table for the thirty-minute ride.

"What was that about? You couldn't hurry up a little?" Hal just looked out the window at the passing English countryside. "And now you're going to ignore me?"

"I guess I didn't sleep that well on the plane."

"Nonsense. I came to check on you and you were completely out."

"What do you mean, you checked on me? What the hell is that about?"

"Look, I needed to make sure everything is set up correctly."

"Damn it, Kate! You know it is!"

"What did you just say!"

"If you're going to talk to me like we're dating, then I'm going to call you Kate."

"Hal, I'm your boss. Remember that!"

"Fine, sorry. We're booked into an affordable hotel. You have a double room; I have a single. A couple blocks away is the Oxford Shuttle, so you can take the bus to Oxford and attend the conference and still escape if you run into someone you don't like."

"You watch your mouth. Is there something going on you need to tell me?"

Hal held his satchel a little tighter.

"Tickets please, everyone." The train steward took the tickets and punched a hole before returning them. He grinned at Hal: "Be nice to Kate."

Hal couldn't look up after that as he could feel Katherine's stare. She let him lead the couple of blocks from Victoria Rail Station to the Premier Inn before stepping in front to check in first.

It was only thirty minutes later when Hal walked back out the front door of the hotel. He'd showered and changed quickly as he had a time limit to worry about. There's a taxi rank outside of the Victoria rail station, and Hal climbed in the first in the queue: "St. Thomas' Hospital, please."

In spite of the afternoon traffic, Hal was soon in the hospital records department and in the middle of a frustrating conversation with a middle-aged woman in the standard starched nursing uniform with a pair of reading glasses on a chain around her neck.

"But I did send an email asking for information, and someone emailed back saying they could not send anything that way."

"That would be correct. We simply cannot send records out that way. If you would like to fill out a form, then we might be able to get back to you."

"After I tried email, I was told to call, but then I was told that nothing could be said over the telephone."

"We take patient privacy seriously here. We cannot, just cannot, answer questions over the phone without the required documentation."

"And that takes me back to what I said when we started talking. I have the required forms filled out right here in my hand, and I'm here in person. Can I please see the records?"

"It takes a great deal of time to go through those records, so I recommend you email a request and see if someone can get back to you."

"All you have to do is get on to your computer. This would only take a few minutes to check."

"My, you are a persistent one, aren't you? What was the exact date?"

"It will be 28 years ago in August."

"Not enough. I need the full date."

"I'm afraid I don't know. I was kind of abandoned as an infant so dates aren't clear. But, there're a limited number of hospitals where I could've been born."

"Really? Oh my, that does change things a little. We take in the charity cases and sometimes, well, they aren't forthcoming with information. But certainly a date would have been recorded?"

"What if she was brought here, you know, a little later, maybe a few hours or even days after I was born, and they didn't know what to write down."

"Yes, that could happen. I don't see anything on the computer records, though."

"Would there be hard copies of the original forms?"

"They're in storage in the basement. Still, I have to warn you that a month and year might not be enough even if something is there. It's also a bit of a mess. What with computers, the print records aren't maintained that much."

"Don't worry. I spent most of my adult life doing research at universities. There's nothing you can show me that I've never seen before."

Hal was soon wondering if that statement was completely true. The records room was clean, and all the written forms were in boxes with storage labels clearly marked. Yet, they somehow seemed incomplete and, with the nurse attending to other duties for a few minutes, he had no one to guide him.

"It's the names. Many of these names are wrong. Here, another Mary Doolittle just like those two files. They couldn't be the same person."

The nurse poked her head in. "Find anything yet?"

"Look at the names. There're three different Mary Doolittles in just one week. How can that be?"

"Oh love, take a look at that code right there on the form. That means it was a charity case, and often she didn't want to give a real name. The nurses would use a name based on the poor girl's accent and other things they figured out. Mary means she was Catholic; Doolittle is Eliza Doolittle from *Pygmalion*. It meant she was an uneducated and probably poor Catholic girl with no home to go back to."

"That I didn't know. Wait a minute; would the last name Wales mean she was from Wales?"

"No, actually the name of a country or city was never used if they wanted to protect their identity. If she was from Wales, the last name was listed as Cymbeline."

"The title of Shakespeare's Welsh play?"

"That's right. Is there anything else here that you have questions about?"

"No, I'm not seeing anything that could help me."

"Have you looked at other hospitals?"

"Not in England. I'm not even sure if this is the right city."

They walked to the front door of the hospital. He nodded and said "Thank you so much for your time."

"Goodbye and God bless. I'll say a prayer you find your mother." The nurse watched him walk away before finding an empty office. There were a few calls she needed to make.

*****

THERE WAS NO NEED for a taxi as Hal decided to spend some time walking. He followed the roadway next to the Thames to his left. He could already see the London Eye, the city's oversized Ferris wheel with the large pods full of sightseers enjoying themselves. He had known it was a long shot, but the anticipation had been destroyed so quickly he was heartbroken. It's one thing to not know about your parents, but it's another to not even be sure where you were born or what your true nationality might be.

Big Ben was across the river not that far ahead, and Hal saw glimpses of the Houses of Parliament. Soon, the area that held the London Eye and the London Aquarium was just across another busy street. He had just made it across the street when a tourist asked him to take a picture. He forgot his troubles as, once he had a picture for one group, another asked him. He used hand gestures to show what direction to move for the best photos as there were several nationalities and all wanted the kind gentleman to help them out.

Nine groups later and Hal finally finished his role as the official photographer to the tourists. It was rather humorous that in three or four of the photos he had taken, a stranger had joined the group. A student last term had told him that it was called photo-bombing. The bomber was so fast that no one in the group could protest, and all Hal really saw through the camera lens was a white Tilley hat like many Canadians own.

He wandered through the area for a few minutes, then stopped to watch the boats on the Thames. The crowds were as thick as they had been only hours before at the Stampede, and the noise became overwhelming. He concentrated on a barge anchored just this side of the bridge. Its once bright orange hull had become a faded allusion to former glory, contrasted by a coil of new rope on the deck. He shuddered, not from the cold but from the mental image of a man struck by a train.

Hal consulted the London city map on his phone and started walking back to his hotel room. Along the way, he regulated his breathing to a steady rhythm and looked in shop windows to focus on things other than recent experiences.

An antique dealer inside the store noticed the stranger looking through the window and motioned him inside. "I see you like the desk."

"I'm a lover of old furniture like this. It's got to be a writing desk from, let me guess, the 18th century?"

"18th it is. It's made from a wonderful mahogany, but we did have to repair the top on it. Someone's child carved their initials and we didn't think it was anyone famous. These desk drawers make a beautiful feature though."

"This is nice." Hal consulted the tag attached to it. "Oh, is that the price? Well I guess that's fair. Mind you, I'm from another country so it's too expensive for me to buy and then have it shipped."

"We have a great shipping cost to Canada. It's a little slow, but it'll get there in great shape."

"I didn't say I was from Canada."

"Really? I could have sworn you did. Maybe it's just because you sound so polite that I assumed you were Canadian. Now, I should tell you that we just have a little problem with the centre drawer not opening all the way. We'll get that fixed up though, and if you're interested it can be fixed quickly. I hear my phone ringing in the back office but feel free to look the desk over and check out our other items."

Hal was soon left alone and ran his hand over the wood, enjoying the feeling of the polished aged mahogany. He opened a drawer and appreciated the craftsmanship that had created furniture that lasted hundreds of years. The middle drawer stuck, and he tried to look inside to find the problem. It reminded him of an old desk featured on an *Antiques Roadshow* episode.

"I know what this is. Hello? I think I know what this is."

There was no response from the back of the store. "Hello? I'm going to fix the drawer." Hal pulled the right-side drawer all the way out and looked underneath the desk. One thing that had been shown on the show was that many writing desks had their own little secrets. The host explained that on this model all you have to do is look for a little piece of wood in a square and push until it depresses. Hal stood and opened the middle drawer completely. "Hello? I've opened the middle door. It was a hidden compartment lock that you had to open."

The back third of the drawer was covered with a small lid. There was a lock built into it but it was obvious it had been broken long before. Hal lifted the top. "Hey, you need to come out and see this. It's a parchment of some sort. I'm going to open this if that's alright with you."

Hal paused and then unfolded the parchment. He didn't move for several moments.

*****

"WE HAVEN'T TALKED much about relationships. Have you had one recently?"

"That's a strange question. Do you mean have I been in love or have I had sex?"

"What about either one or both?"

"Fine, doctor, I haven't had sex in a couple years, you know, since I came here, because I don't really feel like it. Satisfied?"

"What about before you came here? I presume you mean Red Deer and your teaching job?"

"Yes, that's what I mean, and yes, I had sex before moving here."

"You haven't said anything about love."

"You want the full story then? I was in a relationship. It ended badly, and then I got a job offer and came here."

"You've told me a little about your co-workers. Are you attracted to any of them?"

"No."

"The other day you mentioned your boss; what was her name?"

"Katherine."

"Is she pretty?"

"She's a bit of a pain."

"But is she pretty?"

*****

HE PUT THE PARTCHMENT into his satchel and made his way outside, quickly heading towards the hotel while looking over his shoulder every few steps. He wanted to sleep. He wanted to control his breathing, take a handful of pills, pull the blankets over his head and sleep until everything went away.

Chapter 5

"OH, THAT'S JUST WONDERFUL." When Hal had returned to the room he'd collapsed on the bed after being awake for most of the previous 24 hours. Now, with his internal body clock totally screwed, he was looking out the hotel's window at London at 4am.

He sat at the desk and rubbed the sleep from his eyes. There's a silence in hotels that time of day that frequent travellers know about. Most of the guests are asleep as even those with an early flight are still in bed, and cleaning staff have yet to start. Usually that's a welcome respite, but not when you're trying to avoid thinking about something. At this time of day there are no distractions. Instead, you're stuck sitting at a desk in your underwear without any justification for not doing what must be done.

He took the parchment he had found in the secret compartment out of his satchel and placed it on the desk. It appeared to be old parchment that was yellowing with age. The two figures on it were easily identifiable. One was wearing sneakers, jeans, and a tee-shirt. His short hair stood out at various angles as if he were awakened suddenly. The other had straight shoulder-length hair, a small button nose, and full lips. It wasn't just the figures in the drawing that were a problem, it was the setting. The figures were in a room with brick walls and a single bulb hanging from the ceiling by a wire. It was obvious, no matter how many times he tried to deny seeing it, that the figure of Katherine was dead while his was holding a sword.

"Hold on a moment."

Hal put the magazine *True Crime* beside the parchment. The style of the drawing on the cover, even to the untrained eye, was the same as that on the parchment. He switched his gaze between the two drawings several times in rapid succession to compare them and found something in the lower right corner of the magazine cover. Incorporated into the drawing, as opposed to being distinctly separate as many artists would do, were the initials A. P.. Hal examined the parchment and found the same initials embedded into a brick in the wall. It became clear to Hal that the drawings were by the same person. There wasn't anything else he could find of significance, so he put the parchment in the desk drawer.

He could hear the faint sounds of the early morning travellers walking down the hall and decided to give in to a basic human desire: hunger. Outside, he walked the short distance to Victoria rail station before taking the escalator to the top floor where he knew he would find Garfunkels Restaurant. Within minutes, he had whole wheat toast, a small glass container of marmalade, and a pot of tea before him.

As a child, Hal had frightened one of his foster mothers when at age seven she found him trying to read Solzhenitsyn's novel *The Gulag Archipelago.* She had gone as far as to throw out all the books in the house and lock him in his room to keep the devil away. That soon ended when he got the courage to tell a school teacher. He spent the next year in a group home run by a retired librarian who encouraged reading. That year, until she had a stroke and he moved again, was one of his happiest memories. Now, his skill as an avid reader was paying off again.

Terrific Crime was positioned between his toast and his tea so he could eat and read at the same time. He would open a page, place two fingers on the text, and move the fingers down the page. He wasn't reading in the traditional sense, but looking for words or phrases that caught his interest and those he wrote on a napkin. During that period, he was totally absorbed by his task.

Hal spread marmalade on another piece of toast and checked the list he had made and what the words or terms meant. They included "blue cocaine," the nickname for a brand of Canadian beer, and "bunnie hug," which only someone from Saskatchewan would call a hoodie. The magazine was published in Britain, but the content was all Canadian. Hal thumbed through it again. He had read enough work to spot authors' writing habits, and he knew that all of the stories, although attributed to several people including him, had been written by one person.

"So, you're here early, or are you here late?"

Hal looked up at the stranger who had sat at a table beside his, even though the restaurant was nearly empty. "Hmmm, are you talking to me?"

"Well, sure I am, sport. The name's Davey, as in Davey from Dallas, Texas. Let me guess where you're from, shall I? You're not British, but you're digging into that meal like a pro, so I'm going to guess Canada. Toronto, right?"

"Uh, no."

"There you are. I knew it. So, tell me friend, you're here early so I'm betting you had a fight with the little lady. Had to sneak out for a bit? Before you did something you regret? Not that I blame you though; I bet you have good reasons."

"Look, it's a business trip with my, well, boss." Hal looked at the stranger and noticed the slightly greying hair in the sideburns and moustache.

"So, what does she look like, this boss of yours?"

"I didn't say I worked for a woman."

"You're right, friend, but a male boss you can just tell off, not a woman boss. Right? So, what's she like?"

"Well, a little older than me and really smart about academic things. She likes everything done her way, but that's only because administration has to be like that when they're looking after hundreds of students at a college."

"So, friend, you're at a college? And you work for her in what way?"

"She's the English department chair and I teach in the department. No big deal."

"And, come on, what does she look like?"

There was something bothering Hal, but it was taking some time before it became clear. "Long red hair. Kind of thin, I guess. Green eyes. You know, I don't think this is appropriate."

"Oh, she sounds hot, really hot. Now I know what your problem is! You have the hots for her, I bet. Yup, that's it. I bet she knows you have the hots for her all the time and uses you because of that."

Hal looked at the stranger's attire. The suit did not fit that well and was worn at the cuffs. On one lapel, there was a small round metal pin with something that looked like a pen lying across it. "I am not attracted to her; I work for her."

"You know, you should just let her have it, I mean one way or another. Find out if she has the hots for you and go for it. And if not, just let her have it anyways. I tell you that would be brilliant."

"Brilliant? That's an interesting word coming from someone from Texas."

"Oh, Hal, I've been here for a while. So, you know, if your boss is really mean to you, then there's nothing wrong with slapping her a bit. You, know, just to let her know who the boss is really. I bet she'd like it too."

"I would never hit my boss. And I don't think I said my name."

"Fair enough. So why are you both here?"

"We're just heading to Oxford where she's giving a paper on Shakespeare at a conference."

"Lots of talk about who Will really was. I even hear talk about where his corpse wound up. What do you think?"

"He's buried in Stratford-on-Avon in one of the churches. Everyone knows that."

"But didn't they dig him up and move him?"

"It was thought about but didn't happen."

"This boss of yours, I bet she knows. Didn't you say she's talking about him in a couple days?"

"I didn't say a couple days, did I? All I know is what it says in the printed program for the conference. It's something about when William disappeared when he was young. It's not my area of research and I really don't care about it."

Davey's voice changed to a coarse whisper. "But you must know more than that, Hal. Just tell me what Katherine is going to say and nobody gets hurt, no matter what it says in a little story you wrote."

"Who are you!" It was loud enough that others arriving for breakfast noticed.

"I knew you were useless. There're more copies of that magazine, and one way or another this gets settled before she says a word in Oxford." The stranger laid a five-pound note on the table and left before Hal could signal the waitress for his own bill.

By the time he was finished paying, the stranger was long gone. Hal stood at the top of the escalator, watching the movement of the crowds on the main platform heading for the trains taking them around the country. He could see an ebb and flow of those arriving and leaving, and he could sense there was someone who was not moving, but waiting.

Hal returned to the hotel and checked his pockets one more time. He was sure he'd placed the card that opened the hallway door into a shirt pocket, but it just wasn't there. In order to get to all the rooms, guests first swiped their room key card at a security door. Fortunately, it was steps away from the front desk.

"Hi, I appear to have lost my key card."

"There is, unfortunately, a service fee for a replacement. We'll also change the coding so nobody can use the old card to get into your room."

"Fine, I mean, I'm the guy who lost it, right?"

A couple of minutes later and Hal was back in his room. It was a simple layout. There was a large bed, a small computer table, and a doorless wardrobe with two drawers at the bottom for clothing. The bathroom was behind the door a couple of steps to the left. As a result, it was easy to tell someone had been through his belongings. "What'd they expect to find?" It wasn't that things were thrown around the room; it was just that things were a little out of place. It reminded him of what had been happening to his office over the past few months.

Before he went to the main desk to complain, he knew he had to talk to Katherine. He knocked on the door beside his and waited a few minutes before knocking again. He was considering going back to his own room to call her when a chambermaid passed.

"Locked out and the missus can't hear, love? Bet she's in the shower and can't hear a thing. Just don't tell."

She used her master key card to open the door, and Hal stepped in. For a split second, it occurred to him that Katherine might indeed be in the shower or even getting dressed. He didn't hesitate to go into the room.

The bed hadn't been slept in, but her clothing and personal effects were tossed around. He could tell by the layout of papers on the computer desk that she had been sitting at the desk working. He began to imagine her in the room and the movements she would have made. "You were sitting here and then what...the phone...no...the door. Someone is at the door...someone you know...that person enters but there must be others behind. You scream...or try to. You're taken out of here and whoever is left goes through your bags."

He sat at the desk to clear his head for a moment. He had known Katherine long enough to know she believed in her personal safety. Often, when working into the late evening, she'd call campus security for an escort to her car. She had used Hal a couple of times but had a laughing fit the night a cat scared him. She would never open the door for just anyone.

He also knew the way she kept her desk tidy to the point that she appeared to be compulsive. There was something wrong with this desk, and Hal looked at it carefully. The few books she had brought were stacked with the largest on the bottom and the smallest on the top. Notepaper and a pen were just to the left of the books, and the small trash bin had been placed to the left of the desk in the same position as it was in her office. Yet, there was something wrong.

He sat back and stared at the desk before he saw it: a piece of scrap paper used as a bookmark. Katherine only used flowered bookmarks that she purchased at a stationery store. Hal opened the book it was in. In flowing handwriting that Hal could easily tell was Katherine's were two simple words: *Follow Falstaff.*

"What the heck does that even mean? I'm supposed to kill Katherine on Saturday. Today is Thursday. There's nothing about Katherine being kidnapped in the story so something else has happened. Katherine wants me to follow a make-believe character to find her and if I don't then she's dead. Brilliant."

Chapter 6

HAL PUT THE *Do Not Disturb* sign on Katherine's door and, going to his own room, placed a few items into his satchel before heading outdoors again. This wasn't a work of fiction, and he knew that in real life there was something that had to be done. As a result, he was soon in a local police station.

"So, explain this to me one more time."

Hal looked at his watch, surprised at how long he had to wait before a constable even talked to him. "My boss, Katherine, has gone missing and I believe she was kidnapped."

"Did you ask the front desk people if anyone saw her leave?"

"I didn't ask, to be honest. I just thought I should report this right away."

"Of course you did. You also say her room was messy. How often are you in her bedroom?"

"Well, never. You see, she's the chair of my English department. That means she's my supervisor."

"Then how do you know that isn't how she keeps her room all the time?"

"Her office is never messy, and she can be fairly fastidious at times."

"Yes, I see. She didn't tell you she was going out, and her room was messy. I tell you what, if you find any other evidence, like, say, a ransom note or a body, then do come back. We can't even think of looking for someone who missed breakfast. Cheers, then."

Hal was soon on the street trying to think of what he should do next. As far as he was concerned, everything had started when he read the story in *True Crime*. But there was no address, other than London, on the cover. He couldn't find a listing for a phone number or any information about the magazine or the publisher Broken Quill Society online. How else do you find out information about a magazine? That was the dilemma he faced until he saw a coffee shop. The coffee drinkers were well-dressed business people, so he continued down the street until he found a shop where he saw customers wearing sandals and working on laptops. He went in and greeted the barista.

"Hi, could I get the big hot chocolate?"

"You want whipped cream and cinnamon on the top?"

"You bet. Say, I'm looking for the local writers."

"Pick a table. They all claim to be writers. You can take your time because they never seem to leave. And they never tip."

"Hey guys, mind if I pull up a chair and join you? I'm over from Canada for a conference, and I miss hanging out with my local writing group."

"Sit yourself down. I'm a poet, Charlie Gazner, and you may have read my work. I look at common objects as poetical impressions. Did you know that cows eating hay represents the taking of nourishment? Well, it does, and that nourishment becomes the foundation by which a poetical stanza is based. My book is called *Looking Through the Mirror.*"

There was a shout from across the coffee shop: "Ask him how many copies it sold."

"Fifty copies are still better than you ever did, Brenda."

"That's telling me, Chuck. How are ya? I'm Brenda. Have a seat. I freelance write anything from travel articles to how to make a quilt, but my specialty is fiction with strong women overcoming adversity."

"She means erotica."

"Chuck, if you say that again I swear I'm going toss you into the street. Why don't you go back to that post-modernist drivel of yours?" She regained her composure and turned back to Hal. "Anyway, what did you say your name was?"

"I'm Hal, Hal Wales."

"I bet you're familiar with Kafka?"

"Of course."

"What about Kurt Vonnegut, Vladimir Nabokov, or the magical realist Gabriel García Márquez?"

"I've read all their works. Do you write like them?"

"Heck no! They're all men, and they never had any decent female protagonists. Nothing but a bunch of lousy male chauvinistic men if you ask me. No, I write about women who have been stripped of their identity by this phallocentric society that is more concerned about the woman as a baby-making machine than a valuable, equal member of this society. I want my women to stand up and shout their independence at the top of their lungs until they're seen as equals by all these male oppressors. I want them to be forceful. I want them to demand of men rather the traditional role of having men make demands of them. I write like Melody Grace, Lynda Chance, and E. L. James."

"She hasn't had a date in five years."

"Chuck, why don't you grab a bunch of straws and write about how they're a visual representation of a sonnet? Then take it all and run it through a shredder, tape it together, and publish it."

"So what's your game then, Hal?"

"Oh, have to do a lot of academic writing. You know, theory-based things guaranteed to sell half-a-dozen copies. What I really like is writing mysteries."

"Any luck getting published?"

"Not yet."

The writers in the coffee shop immediately lost interest and went back to polishing their prose while Chuck walked to the counter and took a box of straws without the barista noticing.

"That's why I'm here. I wanted to ask if anybody had heard of a publishing company called the Broken Quill Society. They publish a magazine called *Terrific Crime*."

Faces didn't move from the screens.

He knew there was a guaranteed way to get their attention. "I hear they're open for submissions. They're new and trying to fill the next four issues ahead of time."

"Do they pay?"

"Yes, Charlie, and from what I hear they pay a flat rate for poems and a per word rate for fiction."

Brenda waved at Charlie to keep quiet. "What's their contact info?"

"That's what I'm asking. I lost their address, but I know they're in London. I just need some help because being new and all, they're not in the phonebook yet."

Heads went down to computer screens and everyone started with the traditional internet search. Hal peered around heads as various search engines were checked before each writer started looking at blogs and web pages for mentions of Broken Quill Society or *Terrific Crime*. Some sent emails and texts, but all the results were the same.

"I can't find anything. Are you sure that's the right name for the magazine and the publisher?"

"No, Brenda, I'm sure that's the correct name. That's why I'm stuck. I hear they sent a copy of the magazine to my office in Canada, but they didn't put a return address on it."

"No return address? Well, I think we know what the problem is then." Brenda glanced around the coffee shop to a series of heads nodding in agreement. "They used a separate printing company. It's normal; as a start-up magazine, they hired a printing company to keep costs down and that company doesn't check for mistakes of any kind because they don't edit and they wouldn't add a return address if it was missing."

"I get the idea there're many companies that do this."

"Do you know if it's good quality work?"

"No, I was told it was poor quality."

"Then it can only be one company." Heads nodded in agreement. "Let me write this down for you. And Hal, don't have anything to do with a magazine associated with these guys. They look pretty slick, but once they get your money, everything changes."

Hal pocketed the address, and, after finishing the hot chocolate, hailed a cab. There didn't seem to be anything special about the area he was taken to. "So, driver, I'm looking for a book-printing company that's supposed to be here."

"You got it, mate. You just have to go around the back. I won't do that what with there being a seedy crowd in the lane sometimes. You say it's a book-printing company though, how appropriate, mate."

"Why is that appropriate?"

"This used to be known as Grub Street."

It didn't take long to find it. It used to be just a lane with the back doors to shops and a loading dock shared by the business in the building. The shortage of space in London had turned back doors into front doors when the main floor was subdivided. The entrance to Princeton Publishing was next to a loading dock they shared with an internet-based delivery-only flower shop. Hal entered the building to find a desk just steps from the door.

"Well, hello there, sir, and how can I be of service today?" The speaker had a little trouble getting out of the office chair from a combination of a waist size equal to the distance of the chair's arms from each other and the collection of boxes at the chair's casters.

"Hi there. I'm from a college in Canada, and we're looking at having some publishing done here to avoid the mailing costs."

"Then you're at the right place. My name is Nelson, and I can show you around. Let me give you these brochures and cost lists. They're printed here, of course, so you can see our outstanding quality of work. We can do any size job and sometimes, for just a slight additional fee, we can do expedited printing. What did you say you'd be having done?"

"Well, an academic journal is the main idea, but we may look at printing small books as well."

"No trouble at all. Let me show you the presses." He led Hal to a hall window that looked into a small room full of equipment and a half-a-dozen people trying not to trip over power cords. "If you look through this window you can see our three main presses. We can use these to do small journals or any size book, and of course we can do the art for covers at a slight additional fee, and even set up a marketing web site for a slight additional fee. We can even make business cards and announcement cards you can mail to let people know about your most recent publication."

"For a slight additional fee."

"Yes, but take a look at these machines. You just send us a digital copy and it's in the system to be printed right away."

"We had a little idea, though. We were thinking about having a journal done that had an old-fashioned look. There's a magazine called *Terrific Crime* that I think you printed recently."

"I don't know that one, but we have a client base that grows every day, so there's a good chance that a quality magazine would have come from here."

"We kind of liked the way that magazine looked."

"Not a problem; we can print using any kind of font and typeface you want. We can even make a brand-new font just for you for a slight additional fee. Did I mention how many authors publish with us? We list them all on our online bookstore, so we can help sell them for a slight additional fee."

"Well, what we were thinking was, could you do the printing on an old mimeograph? You remember, the machine where you had to make a plate with the text and then pass inked rollers over it a couple times. We want that real authentic old-fashioned look. I don't think the guys back in Canada would worry about a slight additional fee."

"Slight. No, that kind of printing is labour-intensive. It would be a rather large fee, I'm afraid."

"Do you have a mimeograph?"

"It's been a little while, but I'm sure we have one. Let's go this way. Now, you'll note to your left the state-of-the-art storage facility where we keep all our papers and inks in a climate-controlled environment."

"You mean that big closet?"

"On the right, we have a computer-controlled product distribution centre to assure on-time delivery of all our orders."

"You mean the guy at that desk putting a book in an envelope?"

"And this, just behind this door, is our vintage printing presses; we have a wide selection of printing presses for those, like you, who prefer the classical look of their products."

"It's a storeroom of junk."

"If I remember correctly, our beautiful antique mimeograph machine was here. And I don't see it. Well, that's not a problem at Princeton Press because for every problem we can be your solution."

"For a slight additional fee?"

"Let me just ask one of our valuable floor managers who I see coming by."

"He's carrying a mop and bucket. Oh, wait, floor manager. I get it."

Nelson addressed the holder of the mop: "Would you have any idea where the vintage mimeograph machine is? It used to be right here."

"That thing? We got rid of it."

"What do you mean? It was a wonderful vintage printer and just exactly what our customer here wanted."

"The roller didn't roll properly and paper got stuck, and the smell of the ink was enough to make me barf."

"That's still not a problem. I bet we can use our modern machines to perfectly duplicate the mimeograph including, for a slight additional fee, any of the printing errors that a mimeograph would have caused."

Before the floor manager left, Hal managed to direct a question to him over the nonstop chatter of the salesman. "Do you know where it went?"

"No, a couple of guys and a woman showed up and tossed it the back of a lorry."

"You don't know who they were?"

"Nope, they paid cash and off they went. I asked to write down their information for a sales slip and they said just said no."

"Was there anything about them that you remember? I'd really need to get in touch with them."

"Not really, except that the woman had this red hair and a hat with a hatpin that looked like a quill. I remember that because the feather part was purple and was just ugly. Anyway, if you'll beg my pardon, I've got a bit of a mess in the W.C."

Norton hadn't noticed Hal talking with someone else and was still in selling mode. "As I was saying, we can duplicate any form of type and font you desire. Let's walk this way and I'll show you our contracts. We have very affordable contracts, you see, and as you are international, what with being from Canada, a very favourable exchange rate."

"I tell you what we're going to do here." Hal took charge of the conversation. "I'm going to put together a little package of what we need and how we need it done. The mimeograph was going to be an additional fee, but you no longer have one, so we'll have it done on a regular machine at just a slight discount."

"No, I don't think…"

"No, that will work. Now, we are based in Canada and we do prefer to work with Canadian currency. As the exchange rate is a little awkward, we'll all convert to U.S. currency as, I think you'll find, that's beneficial to us both."

"We don't do that."

"Not a problem. Of course, because of the way the Canadian dollar converts to American currency, we would expect just a slight discount in pricing. And, due to the mailing costs being different, we would expect you to cover all of those costs as well. Let's see, we don't need your online bookstore, so we can take that fee off the total as well."

"Oh, I forgot about another appointment. Look, here's the door."

"We really should get this in writing, don't you think?"

"I'll call you later. Cheers."

Hal proudly walked away from the doorway and around the corner to the main street. There was some satisfaction in knowing that the Broken Quill Society had been here and got the mimeograph they used for the magazine. It confirmed the group was real and it was a victory. However, he still didn't know where to go next to find Katherine. He was looking at the London map in case there was a street or avenue named Falstaff when a woman walking by caught his attention. She had red hair and a purple feather hatpin, just as the floor manager had described. He followed her and watched her enter a doorway to a store called The Nom-De-Plume Book Store that had the motto *The Home to Mysteries and More* under its name.

On entering the store, he could see the woman ending a short argument with the clerk before heading down an aisle. Hal picked up a book from a shelf and pretended to read while watching her go through another door at the back of the store and head upstairs. He hesitated as he knew that there would be tenant's apartments on the next floor, which meant he would be entering a private space. The image of Katherine superimposed over a man dead beside railway tracks was enough to make him move.

The numbering on the doors on the second floor indicated there were several apartments. He was attracted to one where there were voices shouting. Before he could think about knocking on the door, it flung open, and he found his legs being hit by the three pre-schoolers pushing past him.

"You go ask your uncle then. You see if he cares what you little rotters have to say. You, it's about time you showed up then. Well, get in here. What are you waiting for? Get in and do your job."

The hat and hatpin were gone, but this was the woman he had been following. He followed instructions and went inside.

"Don't mind those kids; they're my sister's. Little rotters. Anyhow, do it for me before they get back, or there's no living with them. Well, what are you waiting for? It's over there. Fix the bloody thing."

"Sorry?"

"Look, I called you days ago and I need that thing we bought working so I can watch Doctor Who tonight. Easy set up, my sweet hiney."

"Actually, I'm not really here about fixing that. I noticed the pin on your hat."

"Oh, just bloody wonderful. It's one of those shops where they send someone out to see if it needs fixing so they can delay fixing anything until the bloody warranty expires. Not today, you're not. Get over there and fix the bloody telly!"

"Fine." He had no idea why he started to help fix the television equipment. The cables and plugs were colour-coded, so he was easily able to make the connections on the television, DVD player, BluRay player, and a satellite box.

"Would you hurry up before those rotters get back? I already figured out those cables connect to the HD box."

"Well, no, they don't; just look at the colour coding here. About the hat pin, is it a quill, by chance?"

"I almost had this working this morning. Hey, that makes the audio stereo instead of mono so leave it alone."

"You have to switch these to have everything work together. So, could I see the hat pin?"

"If you're the expert, then why do I have to tell you all of this? Look, it's right here in the directions book. At least the part that isn't in Chinese."

"Take your hands off those ones, and let me connect the DVD to the back of this part here."

"Like you don't want my help. Go ahead and show me how bloody talented you are then."

"All done here."

"And about bloody time it is. I can hear the little rotters on their way up."

The door flew open to the weight of the same children, who were then followed by the clerk from the bookstore.

"I told you not to let them come downstairs again. They just make a mess and bother customers, and just who is this standing here, anyway?"

"He's the telly repair man."

"Is he now? Except he doesn't have a uniform or even a repair kit. So, is this who you pick up when I'm not around?"

"What do you care anyway? He fixed the telly so you can watch the footie match this afternoon. And I got some beer and crisps from the Tesco."

"Good. Next time, try to pick up a guy with a little muscle or something. There's no way I'm going to feel jealous looking at that."

During the argument, Hal made his way to the apartment door and went down the stairs and into the store without being noticed. Once on the street, he looked around the street for a cab, but, not finding one, walked a couple of blocks where he decided to rest and get a bite to eat. He stopped at Red's Fish and Chips and, after a few moments contemplating the menu board, ordered the deep-fried herring snacks with beetroot relish and a Dr. Pepper.

"That'll be £6.40, mate."

"No problem. Got some coin in my pocket and a fiver in the wallet, and what's this?"

"What was that, mate?"

"No, sorry, just a note in my wallet, I guess."

"Take a seat. I'll bring the order when it's ready."

Hal sat at a window seat reading the piece of paper from his wallet once again.

How does the soldier stay not known to time?

He guards the door from within for the God

Who lets you repent your oldest known crime

In the Abby where the thousands have trod.

The poem itself wasn't the only problem. The small piece of paper it was written on was folded over a small lock of red hair.

*****

"WHAT HAPPENS WHEN you lose time?"

The twice-daily sessions were beginning to bore Hal as the doctor seemed to take forever in making a point. "How should I know? It disappears, is all."

"Well, you say the amount of time varies, so what happens when it's only a few minutes? Do you go to another room?"

"I was told when I was a kid that I sleep walk, and it's something like that, I guess. I might come to in another room or outside."

"You've never mentioned the sleepwalking before. When did that start?"

"Around the same time as these…"

"Episodes?"

"Sure doc, episodes." The doctor looked at Hal for several minutes before Hal realized what the implication was. "You're saying I was never sleeping. No, no, no, I went to sleep. These, these episodes happen when I'm awake."

"We may come back to that. What about when you lose longer periods of time? Do you know what you do during that time?"

"I come to in different places."

"In the house?"

"No, not always. Sometimes other places. You know…further away."

"That's the real reason you don't drive, isn't it?"

"I've never had a licence."

"Because you knew way back then that something was wrong. You just didn't want to admit it."

Hal looked at his sneakers and nodded.

"Tell me, Hal. Do you ever write during an episode where you black out?"

*****

"HERE YA GO, MATE."

He placed the poem and the hair into his leather satchel and tried to enjoy the herring snacks. Hal washed down one of his pills with a sip of Dr. Pepper and was ready to leave. "Hey Red, where can I get a cab around here?"

"You have to call for one. You know there's a tube stop up the road? You know, what you would call a subway."

"I'm not sure how to get around on the tube."

"There's an app for that."

"Brilliant."

Hal quickly downloaded a phone app with the tube map and information about route planning but knew there was something he had to do. He retraced his steps to the bookstore and found it closed. He looked on either side of the bookstore, knowing that apartments had to have a separate entrance, and found one. The lock, obviously broken for some time, was not a problem, and he made his way upstairs.

"Hello? Hello? I was here earlier. Can I talk with you?"

"Why are you knocking?" The teenager walking out of an apartment hadn't looked up from his phone. "Just go in. Everyone else does."

Hal placed his hand on the doorknob and, feeling his mouth go dry, turned it. "Hello, it's me, the television repair guy. I just need to ask a couple questions." There was still no response, and Hal closed the door behind him. A quick check told him there was no one in the one-bedroom apartment.

He tried to snoop, looking at the top of counters and tables, but couldn't bring himself to open any drawers except for one. He opened the cabinet door under the sink and pulled out the small plastic garbage bin, just like someone does in every detective novel he had ever read.

He looked at it for some time before making himself touch it. It was a wig made of long red hair. Hal pulled it out of the garbage, wondering why she would wear it and just toss it in the trash. He dropped the wig on the floor and took the hat and quill hatpin from the bin. The only thing left in the plastic bin was a piece of paper, and Hal shuddered at the thought it may be another poem. Instead, it was a note: *Payment at 4pm at B. Palace.* Hal looked at his watch and knew where he was going to be that afternoon.

Chapter 7

HE USED THE PHONE APP to find directions on the tube. After spending a half-hour walking the streets around Victoria rail station, and checking his watch repeatedly, Hal found the Shakespeare Pub and headed inside. He settled on a leatherette sofa with a pint of warm bitter in front of him and tried to figure out his next move.

He looked around for a few moments. The bar itself was old, and the 16th century style of printing was used everywhere from the menu board to the notices on the wall, including a sign that said the pub had free Wi-Fi.

There was something he remembered from the Shakespeare classes he had taken as an undergraduate, and Hal began searching online for the location of the Boar's Head. It, after all, was the pub where Falstaff spent a great deal of time drinking. A few links later, and it became apparent that the original pub had been destroyed in the London fire of 1666, and the later version torn down for a new roadway. He reached for his satchel in time to see it in the hands of someone else.

"Thief!" There was no reaction from the pub patrons.

If the thief had seen Hal coming, he might have stepped aside or put a hand out to deflect him. However, as he was facing the door, he didn't anticipate the blow from behind. Both men fell to the floor; Hal grabbed the strap to his satchel. Other patrons watched in amusement as Hal stood. "Nobody steals from me! Do you hear me?"

The would-be thief said nothing but quickly left the pub.

"Not bad." The speaker was a rather portly gentleman wearing a Manchester United jersey. "But remember, cuff him soundly, but never draw thy sword."

Hal was too shaken to pay much attention to him at first, but then he noticed the jersey. "I bet he was a Liverpool fan."

"And you?"

"Man. U. All the way."

"Join the brethren, friend. There's a big match today, and not one of us can afford to get to Old Trafford."

"I can't stay."

"This yours?" The speaker was a barmaid who looked like she belonged on *Coronation Street*, from her cheap permanent to her flowered apron.

Hal took the small metal lapel pin from her and turned it over in his hand a couple of times. It consisted of a circle and a distorted Victorian dip pen in two pieces. It was the same pin he had seen earlier on Davey from Dallas.

"Heya, I've seen that before."

Hal looked up at his brand-new companion, who was having just a little trouble remaining upright.

"There's an office in my building. They have a picture like that that on the door. It's some sort of book company."

"What's the address?"

"Oh, it's over there, somewhere. I don't recall, but it's over there."

"Do you have a business card, maybe?"

"Nope, ran out and can't pay for new ones."

"Do you remember the actual address where you work?"

"Well, no, I just sort of go there every day."

"How about a phone? Is the address on your phone?"

"Oh yes, you bet it is."

"Can you look at your phone?"

"Nope, wife took it. Says I run up the bill."

Hal tried not to show his frustration. "How can I get there?"

"Oh, I'll drive you there later. After the match and all."

"I don't think you'll be in any shape to drive."

"Oh, just you wait. You're staying for the match, right?"

"I think I need to get back to my hotel and lie down for a bit."

"Looks like you need to. Where are you staying?"

"The Premier Inn. It's just over there." Hal pointed in no particular direction.

"Oh sure, I know where that is. I'll pick you up in front, at say, 7pm. Call me Pickels, by the way."

"I'm Hal. Is Pickels your real name?"

"Nope. They call me that because I usually am, you know, pickled. My real name is Toby Belch, but you can understand I hate that name, so just call me Pickels and nobody gets hurt, as they say. I'll see you after the game."

Pickels went back to downing pints with the other patrons while Hal sat in a corner booth for a little longer. He had signed into the free Wi-Fi and was looking up the name Toby Belch to see if he could find a listing for a business address. Hal began to rub his temples, remembering that Toby, or was it Pickels, had said to "cuff him but don't raise a sword." He found the line, "do, cuff him soundly, but never draw thy sword" in Shakespeare's *Twelfth Night*. It was said by Sir Toby Belch. All he could think about was that damn story "The Mystery of Shakespeare's Bones," the conference that the still missing Katherine was going to, and of course the question, a still-there question. Hal heard a rush of dark noise around him and, as he stood to leave, noticed Toby look towards him, smile, and raise his glass in salute.

*****

"HAL, DID YOU HEAR ME? Do you ever do any writing when you black out?"

Hal kept looking at the diplomas on the office wall, reading each in detail repeatedly and saying nothing.

"If I'm going to help you, I need to know what happened in your life."

"Fine." Hal kept looking at the diplomas. "There was some writing that I found when I came around."

"Written by you?"

"I don't know. It was just there."

"What did you write about?"

This time Hal looked at the floor and said nothing.

"Do some deep breathing and then tell me."

The doctor waited, and after a few minutes Hal began to speak. "It was a story about one of my sisters. Not a real sister, of course, but one of the foster sisters I had at one of the homes. She was older than me by a few years."

"What did you write about her?"

"It was about hearing a noise in the night and not doing anything. But it didn't make sense because I remember that one day she wasn't there."

"What happened to her in real life?"

"One day she moved a different home. At least, that's what I heard at first. Then the story changed, and she had run away."

"What was her name?"

"I don't remember."

"What was her name in the story?"

"Ophelia."

There was a long pause before the doctor spoke again. "Hal, what happened to Ophelia in *Hamlet*?"

Chapter 8

IT WAS CLOSING in on 4pm, and within a few minutes Hal was in front of Buckingham Palace near the Victoria Monument. This time, when cameras were held out to him by tourists who didn't speak English, he shook his head no.

Hal climbed as high as he could on the Monument, getting to the same vantage point as tourists. He used his phone camera to try and spot the woman who had worn the wig, but gave up after half-an-hour because of the sheer mass of people.

"So, tell me friend, are you living or just alive?"

"What was that?" Hal looked at the elderly man sitting beside him. He didn't appear to be homeless but was wearing clothes that were well worn and ill fitting.

"Many people go through life just going through the process of being alive and not really living a life at all."

"Well, that's nice and all, but I'm just here enjoying the palace and everything else."

"No, I can tell by the look on your face that you're trying to figure out something serious. It involves a woman, doesn't it?"

"Yes it does, but how would you know that?"

"I'm one of those people who know things about people and how to help them. I can help you live better once you understand how to handle the problems you have."

"No, that's fine; I don't need any help like that."

"My name is Derek Damous, and to answer the first question you're thinking, no I'm not a psychic."

"I'm Hal. So, if you're not a psychic, then how do you know things about people?"

"Hal, let me first ask you some questions. You're sitting here in the middle of the afternoon with alcohol on your breath looking a little depressed. Your clothes are in good shape, so you have a job. You look like a tourist, so you have the money to travel. Why, then, are you depressed and drinking early in the day? It has to be personal, and that's how I know there's a woman involved. Like I said, I'm not a psychic. I'm not going to guess what her name is or anything like that. But I do know you're separated from her and desperately want to reunite before it's too late. Is that right?"

Hal's chest was beginning to constrict. "Yes. It's something like that."

"Then let's take a little walk away from all these people. That park over there is much quieter and relaxing. We can just walk on the paths for a spell."

There were a few minutes where neither spoke and the noise of the tourists behind them faded away.

"Hal, I'll be honest with you. I'm a seer. Not one of those who claim to know everything that's going to happen five minutes after it really happens, but just someone who sometimes knows things that he shouldn't."

"Fine."

"When people stop living, they often wind up in a place where others control what happens around them. Your life is being controlled by others, isn't it?"

"Well, yes, you could say that."

"And those other people have created a situation you can't figure out, haven't they?"

"Yes, I guess you could say that."

"This woman you want to reunite with, she's under the control of someone else as well."

"Yes."

"Let's have a seat on that bench, Hal. I don't normally do this, but I can use tarot cards to help here."

"Wait a minute. You said you weren't a psychic."

"It's not like that. I don't automatically see everything every time. The cards let me focus enough that my abilities as a seer come forward. It's more about me than it's about you."

"Fine then. Let's have a seat."

"Don't look at the literal meaning of the cards as they can mean several things at once." Derek had taken out a deck and was slowly shuffling the cards. "The first card is The Lovers. Now this card, when talking about lovers, often means the person is starting a romantic relationship. However, the card is upside down, which means a relationship is in trouble. It can also mean a problem at work. Hal, this woman you're concerned about is someone you work with, isn't she?"

"Yes. She's my supervisor."

"Then let's try another card. That is, if you'd like to continue."

"Yes, of course. Show me another card."

"We have The Tower this time. Hal, do you have a bit of a temper?"

"No, I wouldn't say that at all."

"You need to understand that sometimes The Tower indicates a temper and stress. Are you under a great deal of stress then?"

"That would be true."

"Watch your temper then, as it could get you into a great deal of trouble."

"Why don't we just move to the next card? How many do you look at, anyway?"

"Just five are enough, Hal. Card three is Judgment. Generally, it means that you reach conclusions too quickly, and that can cause trouble. It also means you're being watched. As we put the cards together, it becomes clear that you're looking for a woman but need to control your temper because people are watching."

Hal closed his eyes for a moment and made an effort to slow down his heart before it exploded. "What's the next card?" The next card was flipped over, and Hal found himself staring at a sword.

"The Ace of Swords."

"I can see it's a sword. The question is, what does it mean?"

"It can mean you're surrounded by people you shouldn't trust. The woman you love might not be right for you, and whatever you do, don't believe things you're told. Hal, something is wrong in your life right now. It's like everyone is out to get you. Look, I can see you're upset, but I'm just telling the meanings here."

"I'm sure you are. Why don't we just call it a day and I'll see you around."

"We need to look at the last card or none of this will make sense."

"I'm not in the mood." Hal went to leave, but Derek put a hand on his shoulder.

"Just one more card, and then we can put everything together."

"Fine. One more card and that's it."

Derek turned the last card over, stood, and began to walk away. Hal jumped to his feet to follow him. "Derek, you were the one who wanted to look at the last card so don't you dare leave now."

"Is that a threat? Are you going to let that temper take control?"

"What the heck are you talking about? What's so special about that last card?"

"It's The Sun." Derek kept walking. "The Sun shows a duality that many people just say is the yin and yang we all have, but I know the truth."

"And what would be that truth?"

Derek stopped and looked at Hal. "It's you. The duality is in you."

"The duality is in me? Fine, then. What does that mean?"

"Put them all together. You're having problems with the woman you work for, and you have problems with stress. It's not that you shouldn't trust other people, it's the other people who shouldn't trust you. That's why you're being watched. I don't know who or what you are, but I know I'd rather not talk with you anymore."

Hal was about to respond when three other men joined them and prevented Derek from leaving. "Well, would you take a look at who it is?"

"Hey, guys, I don't want any trouble here."

"Tell me, Derek, old chum, I can see the cards, so are you still doing your little reading routine?" When he didn't answer, the largest of the gentlemen turned to Hal. "Look, I don't want you to be scared of us; it's just we know old Derek here. Did he do a reading for you?"

Hal spoke rather slowly, not wanting to give away too much information. "Yes, he did."

"Of course, he did. First, he claimed to be a seer, and then he flipped some cards and gave you all sorts of detail about how your wife was going to leave and how you were about to be fired from work. He might have even claimed you were dying."

"Nothing that serious."

"Did he get to the next part?"

"What next part?"

"The part where he tells you he knows how to fix it all, but it's going to cost a fair bit of money for you to get the solutions."

"No." Hal began to glare at Derek. "He got up and ran away, so I had to follow him."

"That's a nice twist." The men turned their attention back to Derek. "Making someone follow you is new. But we warned you before not to con people like this. You don't understand the power of the cards, and you don't even lay them out the way it must be done."

"I saw it this time." Derek alternated between looking at the men confronting him and Hal. "This guy, I saw it, I really did."

"This is going to be good. What was it that you saw this time?"

"The darkness. I saw the darkness in him. There's a woman at risk because he has a secret side the others never see. But I did. I saw it! We have to do something before she gets hurt."

"Come around here again, and someone will definitely get hurt. Give me the cards and get lost, and the next time we see you doing this, we'll take a walk to the river. You'll see how dark things can really get."

Derek turned and yelled at Hal: "I saw it! The tower and the sword are real! You have to follow the darkness before you can find her. I see the sun in the darkness."

"Ignore him. I'm Stefan, and these are my brothers, Loiza and Hanzi. We're real tarot card readers. Derek is nothing more than a pretender and a con artist."

"Really? Some of things he said were pretty good."

"Like what?"

"He knew I have a problem with a woman."

"A guy who has a problem with a woman? Is that a surprise to anyone? You know something, I bet you know a woman whose name starts with a hard consonant sound like a C or a D. Do you know a woman who has a name like that?"

"Yes. Her name is Katherine. How'd you know that?"

"I didn't. There're more female names that start with a consonant than with a vowel. I also didn't say it was the specific woman you're thinking of; I just asked if you knew one with a name that started with a hard sound. Then it's just a matter of following your reactions and I can become just like Derek."

"So this whole thing is nonsense?"

"With Derek, it is. Not with us. Look, here's my business card. You'll find our office not far from here and we're open late. If you stop by, you'll find our services and prices listed just inside the door. We'll give a good discount to make up for everything you just went through with Derek. You might hear what you want to, but at least you'll hear the truth."

Hal put the card in his pocket and walked in the general direction of the hotel. It was another dead end, and Katherine was still missing.

*****

The doctor had shown up at their morning session with a bag of doughnuts and hot chocolate. They spent time chatting about the recent cold snap before the doctor got to the point. "Hal, the foster sister you say you wrote about during an episode…have you thought more about what may have happened with her?"

"I've told you. First, they said Ophelia moved to another home, and then they said she ran away."

"What happened to her in your story?"

"I don't remember."

"Hal, what are you trying to get off your hands? Do you realize you're rubbing them like you're trying to clean them?"

"Look, she disappeared, and then I went to a different school and started grade three."

"Right, grade three. You've been talking like this happened when you were a teenager."

"I was twelve going on thirteen."

"Not if you were going to start grade three. Hal, her file is sealed, but I made a couple of calls."

"So?"

"You started school early and went through grades quickly. You were eight at the time. And her name wasn't Ophelia, it was Jane."

Hal didn't respond, but began to walk around the room, touching anything he could.

"What happened in your story, Hal?"

Hal stopped and looked out the window. "I saved her. People were hurting her, and I went into a room and I saved her."

"You couldn't help her."

"All I had to do was save her. Someone killed her."

"No, Hal. Social services were sending her back to her own home. But they missed some things that were going on there. Something you couldn't know anything about. Things she never spoke about to anyone."

"It was my job to save her!"

"Calm down, Hal. You tried to save her. When they found you, you were still trying to clean the blood off her wrists."

"No! It's my fault! It was my job to save Katherine!"

"Hal, why do you have to save Katherine?"

*****

HAL LET HIMSELF into his room, sat in a corner, and began to cry.

Chapter 9

"MR. WALES? This is the nurse you were speaking with earlier."

Hal had answered his cell phone half-an-hour after entering his hotel room.

"The reason I'm calling is, well, you see, sometimes there are other reasons for a mother not to give personal information…"

"Yes, I'm listening."

"Well you see, at this charity hospital, we deal with the poor and the homeless, but that might not be the only reason for, well, not saying things."

"What would the reason you're thinking of?"

"I don't know if I should really say just yet. I checked with another hospital, and they did have a listing for a child, a baby boy, born at the right time. It's just that the mother…"

"What about the mother?"

"I talked to one of the staff who remembered that night, what with the all the disruptions in the emergency ward and all. And then this woman going into labour."

"Look, I really appreciate that you're trying not to say something, but if this could be my mother then I really need to hear it all."

"It was a theatre group who came in late at night. One of their performances had gone rather badly, and a bit of a mess, a fight with some theatre-goers, had happened. While they were being patched up, a young woman went into labour and had a baby boy."

"That sounds like great news. So, what is it you don't want to say?"

"She was red flagged. By that, I mean, they thought something was wrong, like maybe she was drunk, so they ran a couple of quick tests. But she was clean."

Hal was beginning to sense there was more to the story. "You mean they thought she was on drugs. But if she was clean, there's no problem, right?"

"No. I don't know how to say this, but they red flagged her for a mental health evaluation. They were worried about emotional problems."

"Oh."

"What my friend remembers is that the theatre group she was with were talking about going to Canada to do a tour. She didn't leave her real name, but her friends did. They all left before anyone noticed. I've asked my friend to email some information to you. If you don't want to see it, I'll understand."

"No, I need to see it."

He sat on the bed, and then noticed the envelope shoved under his door. There was no return address on the envelope and no way to tell who had sent it. There was only another poem.

Forgiveness comes for those who try to learn

The battles raged from London town today

To Oxford's shrine that is never to burn

The hero returns with the feet of clay.

Hal placed the poem into the desk drawer with the first one and headed outside.

Earlier in the day, he had been trying to remember something about the character of Falstaff, and it had finally surfaced. Hal consulted the map and got on the train heading for the location of the Boar's Head, the bar where Falstaff liked to drink. He knew the bar was no longer there, but at least he had the feeling that he was following Falstaff.

The motion of the train car was comforting, and Hal closed his eyes. Katherine's image was softened by the sunrise in a prairie sky. Her red hair, on fire, reflected the rays of warmth. The sky darkened just before he shoved a sword into her bosom.

Someone stepped on his foot and Hal woke quickly enough to realize it was his stop. He found himself on the street looking at rows of three-storey buildings, each more mundane than the last. It appeared that the top floors were apartments, and the bottom two offices of various types. There was nothing notable in the window fronts to indicate where he needed to go, so he walked up and down the same three blocks several times.

Hal saw something familiar and jogged across the street. Inside the small Tesco grocery store, he looked for a stock boy who was bored. "Excuse me, I'm a little lost."

"Down that aisle and the first door to the right." The stock boy continued filling a shelf with bars of soap.

"I don't need a bathroom, thanks. I'm looking for a business called Broken Quill or maybe Broken Quill Society."

"Is it one of those charities raising money for people living on the streets?"

"No, I don't think so. They're a kind of publisher."

"Never heard of it."

Hal decided to try one more thing. He went to the wine and alcohol section, which was watched over by a store security guard. "Hi, do you know where Toby Belch works?"

"Who? No. I've never heard of someone like that."

"Oh. Wait a minute. What about Pickles?"

"Now Pickles I know. In fact, we all know him. I had to throw him out of here just last week."

"Where can I find him?"

"There's a footie match on, so probably in a pub somewhere."

"Do you know where he works?"

"Sure, right across the street where you see the orange awning over the door."

Hal hurried back across the street. There a security panel beside the door that must have been a nice feature when it worked.

Now, it was a discoloured rectangular piece of brass inset with brass buttons. A quick trip up the stairs and he saw a sign on an office door: The offices of Toby Belch, MD. Podiatrist. Further down the hall was another door with cheap peel-and-stick lettering. Several letters had been removed in haste and all that was left was *ken Qui.*

He used a single finger to open it wider. Inside he found two antique writing desks and chairs as well as the missing mimeograph machine. One desk had several copies of *Terrific Crime* on it.

Hal opened the drawers on the desk holding the mimeograph machine and found the middle drawer only opened halfway. Instinctively, he removed the right drawer and checked for a lock mechanism. Within moments, he had opened the concealed compartments in both desks and held two drawings of himself killing Katherine. He recognized the style and the initials A.P. were the same as that on the drawing he already had.

The squeak of the floorboard just behind him was faint, but still loud enough that Hal ducked and moved to the left to avoid the blow meant for the back of his head. He moved to the other side of the desk before facing the man who had tried to rob him that afternoon.

"You know," Hal was trying to think as fast as he did when bullies were out to get the smart kid in junior high, "I called the police before I came here."

"Bullshit."

It wasn't the single word reply or even the way it was said that worried Hal the most.It was the grin showing perfectly white teeth that bothered him. "Before they get here, just tell me where Katherine is."

"No."

Hal watched his opponent open a desk drawer and remove a small letter opener. "Did you do the drawings? They're really good."

"Thanks"

Hal noticed the arms relax, although the letter opener remained in one hand.

"So, this is where the magazine was made?"

"Ya."

"What happened? Someone mail it out too soon?"

"Ya."

"What happens now?"

There was no response. Instead, the grinning man played with the letter opener.

"But this isn't in the story, right? I'm supposed to kill Katherine, and I can't do that if I'm dead, right?"

"Her? Too late."

Hal managed to place a foot on the desk behind him with enough force to propel himself towards his assailant. It's one thing to tackle someone with his back to you, but a face-first attack is different. Hal was grabbed by two strong arms and thrown towards the corner. His left side absorbed most of the force, and, by the time he regained his feet he found a very sharp letter opener near his throat.

"You love her?"

Hal said nothing, but looked at the hand holding the opener. He was shoved hard against the wall.

"I said, you love her?"

"Yes! Dammit, yes! Now tell me where she is!"

He didn't turn away from Hal, but stepped back, shuffled through several papers, put one near the edge of the desk, and slammed the letter opener in it to hold it in place. With that, he left the office and Hal could hear his footsteps going down the stairs.

Moments later, Hal was on the street, holding a drawing on a piece of parchment.

"Oh my, isn't that just lovely?" The woman who had spoken to him was barely five feet tall, extremely elderly, and wearing a matching tweed skirt and blazer. Her flat-topped, wide-brimmed hat looked like it was from *Anne of Green Gables*.

"I'm sorry?"

"That is an absolutely lovely drawing, young man. Is this your work?"

"Ah, no, not at all. I was just given it, and really I don't know what it means, or is, I guess would better to say."

"You sure aren't making much sense, young man. Are you feeling alright? You're not one of those drug people, are you?"

"No, no, nothing like that. It's just that, well, I need to find someone, and this was given to me as, well, like a scavenger hunt."

"That still made no sense. You do know what kind of bird that is, don't you?"

"No, no, I'm afraid I don't."

"It's a Microcerculus ustulatus."

"A micro what?"

"Oh, young man, when will they go back to teaching Latin in schools? I have to tell you that in my day we could recite classic poems the way they were meant to be read, and if we didn't, the nuns would take out a ruler and redden our hands."

"Sorry, sorry about that. Could you tell me what a silly Canadian would call it?"

"Canadian? Well that does explain a great deal. You Americans would call it a Flutist Wren."

"Thank you so much for helping, but like I said, I'm Canadian, not American."

"Young man, the last time I checked, Canada was on a continent called North America. Therefore, you're American. Or have you moved the country recently?"

"No, but it's not the same."

"Perhaps to you living in the colonies; however, those of us who received a proper British education will always see you as American."

"You realize that we used the Union Jack until the '60s? The head of Canada is the Governor General who acts as the Queen's representative. Isn't that British enough for you?"

"Your Governor General isn't appointed by God to serve for life like a proper royal. As for that flag you love to wave while we beat you at curling, how wonderful that you put a leaf on it instead of being creative. Now, if you'll excuse me, I think I hear a Dartford Warbler."

As she walked away, Hal took another look at the drawing. "A wren? What's so important about a Wren? Wait a moment. I think I get it now."

He knew that in Shakespeare's era, Eastcheap was a food market that had later burned to the ground, and Christopher Wren was the architect hired to rebuild it. When he'd finished, he also built a monument to the Great Fire. Hal began to run the three blocks in that direction, realizing the tube stop he had used was called Monument after the tower.

Hal soon stood beside the front of a small booth where tickets to climb were sold when the London Memorial Tower was open for tourists. Right now, though, there were signs describing a renovation underway and orange tape that was not to be crossed. But thanks to a metal mesh security door that been pried open, he was able to peer into the dark interior.

The circumference of the tower should have been a warning of how narrow the inside curved stairwell was going to be. The first thirty steps were easy enough. At the end of the next thirty, he had slowed considerably. The steps were not as high as a regular staircase, but their depth varied depending on whether you climbed the inside or outside of the tower.

At around 120 steps he stopped completely. Like many tourists not used to sea level, he was having trouble keeping his breath. There's no real way to climb the tower taking multiple stairs at a time as the diameter of the tower makes that impossible. Hal had to shuffle to make sure he didn't trip.

A door slammed well above him.

"Katherine!" Hal attempted to sprint the remaining stairs, keeping to the outside where they were deeper. "Katherine! Are you there?"

Between the dim light and the turning staircase, he didn't see the push to his chest coming. The blow pushed him against the outside wall, where he found it impossible to keep his balance as someone ran past. He grabbed at one of the small windows, trying to find a handhold in the indentation, but he tumbled down twenty steps. As he lost momentum, he found himself lying against the rough outside wall.

"Move again, and I will take you out!" He could see the backlit outline of a person holding something over their head. The voice was, fortunately, highly recognizable.

"Katherine, Katherine, ease up. It's me."

The silhoutte swung the object back a little further to gain momentum.

"Kate, it's me, Hal."

"What did you call me? Is that you, Hal? You're one of them! I'll take you out, I swear."

"No. I'm here to help rescue you, really."

"Does it look like I need help?" She dropped the crowbar and helped him to his feet.

They soon stood outside of the Monument looking at the damage done to the security door. "I guess this is normally overrun by tourists, but it's closed for a couple days for renovations."

"Yes, Hal, that's what the sign right there says. You want to tell me what's going on? Some guy wanted to throw me off the top of this thing."

"Do you know something about Shakespeare that's hidden?"

"Are you sure you're not one of them? They asked the same question over and over. Enough of this shit. Take me to the hotel."

"And then we'll find the police station and report everything."

"You think?"

"I'm just trying to help."

"If you want to help, then go in that shop and get me a coffee."

Hal did as he was told and stood in line for her favourite dark roast blend.

"Hey, is that Kathy you're talking with outside?" The barista was smiling broadly.

"You mean Katherine? How do you know her?"

"I was at the same pub she was last night. Can she ever dance up a storm! And those guys she was with couldn't stop smiling. I mean, she's still wearing the same clothes she was wearing then."

"Tell me about those guys."

"Oh man, are you the boyfriend or something? Hey, I didn't mean nothing by it. I just meant she looked ready to party. Dance, I meant ready to dance."

"I guess dancing isn't that bad."

"What she really wanted was to go up that tower." He pointed in the general direction of the Monument.

"Really?"

"Ya, she was mad 'cause it was closed up for a couple days. I told her I worked by it and might be able to sneak her in, but it looked like the other guys beat me to it."

"Interesting."

"If you're not her boyfriend, can you put in a good word for me? Maybe give her my number."

"You're not her type."

"And what is her type? A couple strangers at bar? Tell her Bennie the barista says hi."

Hal paid for the coffee and went back to Katherine. "Dark roast with two sugars and no cream."

"Thank you."

"So, I hear you like dancing."

"What're you talking about? Never mind. Go get me a taxi."

"We'll take the tube, and on the way, you can tell me all about dancing at a club last night. Oh, and Bennie says hi."

It wasn't until they were seated on the train that Katherine offered an explanation. "It wasn't a club, it was just a pub, and I just danced to a couple songs."

"Then how'd you go from dancing to being in a tower wearing the same clothes an entire day later?"

That comment got the attention of several young men within earshot, but the look Katherine gave them was enough warning that they went back to texting friends. "Hal, listen to me carefully. This is not one of your short stories; this is real life. All I did was dance to a couple of old Eurythmics songs the band played."

"Do pubs have bands? I thought that's only clubs, which is why people say they're going clubbing."

"Whatever. I danced to a couple of songs, and then things went a little hazy. Look, as soon as I get changed, I'll tell everything to the police, alright?"

"You sound pretty defensive to me."

"And why shouldn't I be? Someone just tried to kill me. And don't you dare say I had it coming."

"I didn't say anything of the sort."

*****

"DO YOU REALLY like Katherine or not?"

"Damn it, doc, let it go!"

"Hal, for me to help you, I need to know everything."

"She's my boss and a major pain."

"But?"

"There was one time I saw her late, you know, when she was on a date wearing this little black number."

"Lovely long legs?"

"She's shorter than me, so no. Just the most wonderful red hair. What the hell does it matter, anyway?"

"You seem to want to defend her. Why is that?"

"Maybe I want to be her hero. How's that?"

"Or maybe, Hal, you hurt her in one of your stories?"

"No."

"When you had an episode?"

"No."

"Are you sure?"

"Doc, the most stories I wrote when I blacked out was about finding my mother."

"None about Katherine?"

"Those I wrote when I was awake."

Chapter 10

"SO, HERE IT IS. Earlier, you, Hal, is it? Came here to report that you, Katherine, must have been kidnapped." The police constable was shuffling several papers. "Because, if I can read this writing, her room was messy."

"You went into my room?"

"I had to see if you were there. It was obvious someone had searched your bags, so I made a report."

"Things are getting rather busy tonight, so Katherine, let's hear your story."

"Officer, you need to understand that Hal doesn't always understand what's going on around him."

"Katherine, that was rude of you. I knew something was wrong, so I went looking for you. If I hadn't gone into your room, I wouldn't have known you were missing."

The constable held up a hand to gain control. "I'm asking the questions here. Katherine, are you saying you weren't kidnapped then? Did anyone search your room?"

"Well no, I just was in it to wash up before we came here, and nothing was wrong or missing."

"But Katherine, there were things all over the place."

"Hal, I was unpacking, that's all."

"Would you two stop the lover's spat and tell me something about a crime before I give you both the boot."

"First, officer, we're not lovers, just colleagues.

"Get on with it!"

"I'd made arrangements to meet a couple of people for drinks yesterday evening. I didn't tell Hal because…well, because I didn't have to. Look, I went out with them, but something happened."

"Of course you knew them?"

"Yes. No. Sort of. We'd talked on the internet about researching books for some time, and they sounded like a good couple of guys to have as professional contacts. After two or three drinks, everything went black, and I woke up on a sofa."

"What were their names?"

"Well, one was Sammy."

"And the other one?'

"Honestly, I don't remember his name."

"How'd you have contact with them again?"

"We emailed each other."

"Then you should have names on the email."

"About that, his email address name was SammyActs. But he knew all sorts of interesting things about Shakespeare, so I knew he was really an academic."

"Interesting. Continue."

"You need to believe me, officer, nothing happened while I was unconscious. But when I woke up, they wouldn't let me go, and they interrogated me about my research."

"What is it you research again?"

"William Shakespeare. I think I told you that already."

"Oh yes, we have plenty of these cases. Come Saturday night we'll investigate several cases where Shakespeare fights with Elvis."

"I have no desire to be talked to like this. I want a supervisor in here now, and I want someone from the Canadian consulate, and I want…"

"Calm down. They wouldn't let you go, and that's a crime. Anything else?"

"I blacked out again and when I came to we were in the London Monument. I think he was going to throw me off the top."

"Which one?"

"Sammy."

"Where was the other gentleman?"

"How should I know?"

"Interesting. Well, you've given me the first name of one of them and we'll look at the office that Hal spoke of earlier where, what do I have here, you confronted a man who draws pictures of Katherine and birds. How fascinating. I have to warn you, nothing may come of this."

"So you don't believe me, then."

"I didn't say that, but I need to be honest. You went for drinks with two men you'd never met before and woke up in their flat. If you passed out again, then you can't be sure if they were refusing to let you go. They may have been concerned about your safety if they let you leave while you were drunk."

"And throwing me off the tower?"

"The top of that tower is enclosed by heavy mesh, so nothing can be thrown off. I'll put in a request to check the CCT; that's our security cameras for you yanks.

"We're Canadians."

"Yes, that's such a big difference. However, if CCT footage shows that you helped break into the tower, then you'll be back in here. Breaking into a heritage listed property is a serious crime in England."

"So nothing will be done?"

"I have the name of the hotel you two are staying. We'll get back to you if we learn something."

With the police interview over, the pair walked in the general direction of the hotel before stopping at a MacDonald's.

"I can't believe the way that cop treated me." Katherine was speaking in between bites, and Hal was rather surprised bu how quickly her hamburger was disappearing. "And you, what were you doing going into my room?"

"You weren't answering the door."

"So you thought you'd just let yourself in? What if I was in the shower or getting dressed? What then?"

"Then I guess I'd have to poke my eyes out with the traditional sharp poker."

"Oh, don't be smart with me."

"You know, if I hadn't found you were missing, then I never would have looked for you. What would've happened then?"

"Well, they sure couldn't have tossed me from the tower, or didn't you hear what that cop said?" She began to concentrate on finishing her fries four and five at a time. "Why are you looking at me like that?"

"I'm just, well, admiring your hair."

"Sometimes I have no idea what you mean. Are you finished? Look, I'm too jazzed to go to sleep, so why don't we go for a walk. I'm just so pissed right now I could kill someone."

Hal held up one finger as he was checking his phone. The file that had been sent was a scanned photocopy of a nurse's report. He knew he would send a thank you reply later, but right now all he could do was enlarge the few sentences in the middle of the document saying that the woman, meant to be held for observation, had disappeared with her newborn son. She had been in the company of a group known as The Queen's Men.

"Do not wave that finger at me again."

"I need to check something."

"What you can do is get walking, or would you rather I walk by myself? Some hero you are. Like I said, I could kill someone right now."

"Katherine, you're not the only one."

Chapter 11

"NO, I DON'T WANT to see the map on your phone, Hal; just keep moving. I told them I wanted to go, and they just kept asking me stupid questions about what I'll say on Saturday. At least Sammy did. The other guy just sat there in the background. And nothing sexual happened by the way. Thanks for asking."

"You sound disappointed."

Katherine was aiming for his face but hit his shoulder. "Oh, shit, sorry."

Hal stretched his arm to relieve the ache. "That's fine. I'm sure you meant to."

"You mean, I didn't mean to."

"Whatever floats your boat."

She hadn't heard. "Hal, what's that up ahead?"

"It looks like some sort of tour. Oh, it's a ghost tour." He stopped walking so quickly he almost lost his balance. The sign welcoming everyone to the start of the tour became visible as people moved: *The Ghosts of Victoria Walking Tour: Find the Darkness Within.*

"Welcome, everyone. If you haven't yet, just come to the table as it's only a ten pound note, and that includes the tax."

Hal nodded and Katherine paid.

"My name is Robert, and I'll be your guide for the night. As I hear Big Ben striking midnight, let's begin our tour."

The others on the tour were middle-aged or older tourists, and many had just come from a late theatre performance. But they all wanted to see everything before having to head back to their home countries.

"How many of you have seen the movie *Braveheart* starring Mel Gibson?"

Most people raised their hands.

"Before being drawn and quartered, he was paraded through the streets. It was on this location where a red-haired woman came out of the crowd and gave him a beer. When he was finished, he asked for a kiss, and she obliged. He then proclaimed that he would return to this spot and kiss the first red-haired woman he saw. Is there a red-haired woman amongst us tonight?"

The group looked at each other before they all settled their gazes at Katherine. "Ah, my dear, might Sir William be interested in placing a kiss on your lips?"

"If he did," Katherine grinned slightly, "then Sir William should expect a swift kick in the groin."

Robert used the laughter to his advantage as he listed facts and told stories to keep his group entertained while they walked to various locations.

"Sometimes I can only tell you the story and not show you the actual building. Where this Tesco now stands used to be a house used for boarders for many years. When they tore it down about five years ago, they found a body in the wall. The peat used as part of the basement foundation mummified the body so well that they could still identify it. You may have heard of the phrase "kill all the actors." Well someone really did it. They identified the corpse as an actor who had just finished a run playing the lead role in *Henry V*." Hal held the satchel tighter. In it was the book he had found in the yellow house in Calgary where the bodies of actors had been found.

Hal could tell some in the crowd were getting restless and, clearly, so had Robert. It came as no surprise to Hal that on next block Robert tried a different approach. "Now many of you have no doubt heard of places in the world where there's a fracture between the worlds of the living and the dead, allowing ghosts to come through." He had stopped on what appeared to be a regular street lined with three-storey row housing. "This is one of those places. Just stand still and keep looking in this direction because if you look right at them they won't come through. When they feel safe, they'll move down the street, and you can often feel them on the back of your neck."

"I feel it!" "Me too, I feel it." Soon most of the group jumped in to claim they felt something touch them.

Katherine nudged Hal. "The way the buildings are here, this must be a bit of a wind tunnel effect."

Hal licked a finger and surreptitiously raised it. "Yes, but don't tell anyone. They're having too much fun."

Robert took them around a corner. "This is a disturbing place to visit." He surveyed the group, making sure he had their attention. "This was the home of Elizabeth Brownrigg. That might not be a name you recognize immediately, but in the mid-1700s she became well known. Elizabeth gave birth to sixteen children, although only three survived. She was also a midwife who earned a job at the London Foundling Hospital."

Hal listened intently but looked directly at a crack in the pavement so nobody could see his eyes.

"The Foundling Hospital was not what you would think of as a hospital today. The word *hospital* meant hospitable as children were welcomed there. Parents who couldn't feed yet another infant would drop the child off before they had their first birthday. The children were sent to wet nurses until around five and then returned to the Foundling Hospital to be trained for employment."

Hearing that, Hal relaxed.

"And then you have Elizabeth Brownrigg showing up at the hospital. She was given a nice place to live and young teens to be her servants. And that was a mistake. Elizabeth would strip the servants, tie their hands to beams or posts, and whip them."

There were various shouts and Robert had to wave his hands to keep control. "The authorities learned about this when one of the girls escaped, so they told Elizabeth's husband to better control his wife and that's all they did. One of the girls, who was only fourteen, died from infected wounds, and Elizabeth was charged with murder and put to death."

The crowd was still upset, but Robert knew how to pacify them and still entertain. "She wasn't the only person to abuse servant children back then, but after she was executed, the public demanded something be done and laws were changed. She still visits this location looking for another child, a foundling who she can take to her kitchen, tie to a ceiling beam, and beat to death."

Cries of "no" as well as laughter came from the group.

"They say when she was charged, Elizabeth keep claiming that it wasn't her but a darkness that came over her who was really responsible. Some claim that she had a split personality while others now say that the darkness meant she was under the power of the devil. Many agree, though, that Elizabeth Brownrigg was a seriously mentally disturbed woman."

That was all Hal could listen to and he grabbed Katherine, mumbled something about being tired, and headed in the other direction. He insisted they walk quickly for a few minutes.

"I don't know what your problem was, Hal. I was having fun."

"I don't like hearing about children getting hurt."

"Oh, that was a long time ago. Where do we go next?"

"Turn on this street."

"I'm glad you were paying attention."

"Sort of."

"Sort of? We're lost, aren't we?"

"No, Katherine, I'm using the phone to check the map. None of these streets are straight, and I can't see more than half a block at a time."

"Which is another way to say we're lost. We were with a perfectly good tour, and you insisted we walk away without knowing where we are, and now we're lost."

"Fine. Why don't you wave your wand and tell me where we are?"

"Are you saying I'm a witch?"

"Well, if you're asking…"

"Hey! Hal, I know that place. Sure, that's The Constitution. That's the place I was at last night."

As they approached, they could overhear the bustle from the patio but decided to go inside. "Kathy, how nice to see you again. I think we have a little table in the corner." The server continued to smile as she took them to the table. "So, Kathy, would you like another whisky and beer chaser?"

"The name's Katherine and, no, just a white wine and a little information."

"Wine it is. And for you sir?"

"Just a Dr. Pepper if you have it."

"Oh, you must be the boyfriend."

"No, I'm not her boyfriend."

"My bad. Last night Kathy told me her boyfriend had a little Dr. Pepper addiction."

Katherine clearly wanted to put a stop to this conversation. "We're co-workers and that's all. And the name is Katherine."

"Yes, I remember. It was Katherine when you came in the door and Kathy after a couple drinks. Speaking of which, here they are."

Hal was impressed. "How'd you do that? You didn't even go to the bar."

"We're on record as having the fastest service anywhere. Really, all I do is tap your order into this phone, a bartender puts it together, and a runner brings it over."

"Don't you just love technology?"

"It's made my life easier. What about you?"

"I'm an English professor, so my students submit their work electronically, then I just mark it and return it the same way. It saves a great deal of time I can spend doing other things."

"I like spending time doing other things."

"If you two are finished flirting…" Katherine was glaring. "I wanted to ask a couple of questions."

The server wrote her name and number on a napkin and slipped it to Hal. "Ask away Kathy, that is, Katherine."

"The men I was in here with, are they regulars?"

"No, I can't say I'd seen them before."

"One of them was named Sammy, but I can't remember the other's name. Would you recall?"

"No, I can't say I do."

Hal decided to try. "What she's trying to ask is, do have any idea who she was here drinking with last night."

"Oh, you did have a good time, didn't you?"

Katherine kept her voice even. "What my employee is concerned about is that I may have, that is to say, I left something…"

"She left her purse at their place and needs to get it back but can't remember where they live."

"Hal, that's not true at all. I just need to get in touch with them. About something. And it doesn't matter what." She drained her wine glass.

The server was turning red as she controlled a laughing fit. "I wish I could help you, but we just get too many people in here to watch them all."

"Alright then. Thank you. Hal, I need the bathroom and then we'll be leaving."

The server pointed Katherine in the right direction before turning to Hal. "Sure seems like you two are dating to me."

"Oh, no, but tell me, do you have dancing here?"

"Now that's a good question. The band plays downstairs in what we call The Cellar. But there's no dance floor."

"I'm just asking because Katherine said she went dancing."

"She was dancing alright. If you call what she was doing, dancing. I tell you she was right out of it, so those two guys had to haul her out of here."

"What'd they look like?"

"Want to pay them a visit? You're sounding like the boyfriend. One was older with a full beard and the other was younger. Kept drawing pictures. I just can't remember that much about him. Oh, look who's back."

Katherine stared at her intently. "Do me a favour and call us a taxi."

Hal held up his phone. "I have directions right here."

"Think again, Magellan; I just asked somebody and found out we've been walking in the wrong direction half the night. Make sure you get a receipt for those drinks, so we can put them on an expense account."

Twenty minutes later, Katherine sat in the chair in front of Hal's small computer desk. "I'm still not impressed by that cop. Something is wrong here, so I think it best if I stay in this room tonight."

"Sure, we could change rooms."

"No, we can share this room, so go pick up some of my things from mine."

"When I realized someone had gone through my stuff, I went to the front desk and got a new room card with a different setting so the old one wouldn't work. You can pop downstairs and do the same."

"So, you didn't think of getting my card changed at the same time. How nice of you. Go get my things."

"But, if we're not going to change rooms then, well, where do I sleep."

"Are you still standing there? Go get my things."

Hal soon reappeared carrying an assortment of cases and books which he neatly tried to put on the bottom part of the open wardrobe.

"Oh, just throw them down. It's not like you can hurt a suitcase. I'm just so angry at the police, I could scream. I could also scream at you for going into my room and looking at my things."

"I was trying to help."

"Of course you were trying. Emphasis on the word trying. By the way, how'd you just happen to be at the Monument? I find that rather convenient."

"I found the clue you left."

"What clue?"

"Remember the note? Follow Falstaff?"

"I didn't leave that as a clue. I was going to throw you a bone after the conference and give you an idea for your next book. It sounded like your kind of title."

"An insult? Really? I spent all day looking for you after I found that. I found you in Eastcheap."

"Alright then, that's almost interesting, but I'm too tired to care right now. I'll sleep under the comforter, and you sleep on top. Problem solved."

"You know, I might have wanted to go out for a drink."

"Lie down and go to sleep."

"That cute server gave me her number."

"And I should care?"

"The note under it says to give it to you when you feel better."

There was a long pause. "Do me a favour and be quiet."

*****

"FROM WHAT YOU'VE SAID, many of the current episodes have to do with you looking for your mother."

"Well, doc, we've already talked about that." Hal had been out of his voluntary commitment for some time and was watching the spring thaw through the office window. "It's causing me stress and that causes my brain to splinter a little. But those pills you gave me stopped that."

"Hal, there are three important women in your life. The first was your foster sister. She died. One is Katherine, and don't wave your hands at me like that. She may be a pain in your ass, but you are attracted to her in some way we can figure out later. The important person for you right now is your mother."

"I was thinking that maybe I should just stop looking. Looking caused all these other problems, so why bother?"

"No, you really need to find her."

"So I can resolve my stress?"

"Well, that, and something really important."

"What?"

"This condition of yours…"

"What about it?"

"It's often hereditary."

Chapter 12

SLEEP COMES QUICKLY when danger has been removed; at least, that's the theory. Long after Katherine's breathing became regular, Hal's eyes were open. Images from the day were melted, thawed, and resolved into something new in the hopes of finding reason in the chaos. A quill, its tip worn from use and stained by ink, was broken and discarded by its user. A book containing secrets was thrown into the ocean. A pressure on his chest restricted airflow for a few minutes. Hal was uncertain if he wanted to move Katherine's hand. That thought caused another half-hour of staring at the ceiling before his eyes finally closed.

"Creep!"

The hand slapped him so hard that he tasted blood on the inside of his cheek. His eyes flew open, and he saw the next slap coming.

"You creep! You're one of them, aren't you?"

Hal attempted to move before he was struck again, but was tangled in the comforter. The magazine was shoved under his nose. "Try to deny this. It's right there that you're going to kill me." Katherine leaned forward so she was almost nose to nose with Hal. "Are you planning to kill me? Don't try to lie. You're no good at lying."

"Katherine, I'm not going to kill you. You need to believe me; I didn't write that story."

"So, it just magically appeared with your name on it? Not to mention all the details it has about me having sex with you. Do you think I want to?"

"Well, I was thinking about that."

"About me having sex with you. You goddamn pervert!"

"No, not the sex part. The who wrote it part."

"And?"

"Do you remember a few weeks ago when I told you someone had been breaking into my office at night?"

"Oh, that's right. Your Star Trek toy wasn't where you left it, and the cleaning staff hadn't been in that night at all."

"It's a replica, not a toy. And a sonic screwdriver is not from Star Trek. I'm a Whovian not a Treckie. Yes, someone broke in and moved things around."

"Really? Are you suggesting that someone went into your office in the middle of the night and wrote a story about you killing me? And the cops were laughing at me. Tell me, Hal, why would anyone in their right mind do that."

"Maybe they want to frame me."

"That's just lame. Oh, boohoo, someone wants to frame you. Well somebody tried to kill me! All you did was just show up claiming I left you a clue."

"I've explained that."

"You must know something. Who were those guys?"

"You were the one who went dancing with them, remember? And would you move so I can get up."

"Don't put that on me. You must know what's going on."

"No, I don't. I mean, I'm getting an idea, but I really don't know everything. Would you stop hovering over me like this?"

"Did you just look down my blouse? This is just like the story, isn't it? You want to seduce me, don't you?

"No!"

"I saw your eyes! You looked down my blouse."

"No, I mean, well, no."

"Did you like what you saw?"

"Well, no, I mean, well, if I looked, I would have, but I didn't."

"You didn't like them?"

"No, I mean, I did, but I didn't look."

Satisfied, Katherine stood up straight. "Have a shower and make it fast. We have a problem to work out. And change your clothes; you're beginning to smell."

It wasn't long before they made their way to the restaurant on the Premier Inn's lower level.

"You know, the breakfast is pretty good for a budget hotel. You have to try the blood pudding."

"I don't think so, Hal. In fact, you should have asked for the granola and yogurt."

"You mean the baby food and the stuff ducks eat. I don't think so."

The pair finished their meals in silence.

"Alright, Hal, what is it you think you know?"

"I can tell you, this seems to be about what you're going to say tomorrow."

"There's nothing special about it, Hal." Katherine's grin was enough to indicate she was lying. "It's nothing really that important unless you're looking at making the biggest announcement academia has seen in the past one hundred years, that is. I just happen to know where William Shakespeare was during his lost years."

"He disappeared for the first time when he was what, 14 years old?"

"You got it. You need to understand I spent years on this research. I travelled all around England and Europe and slowly put the pieces together. Imagine, if you would, a giant jigsaw puzzle with half the pieces missing, and every time I found one, I'd know where to look for the next one. You've never done anything like this."

"I've done plenty of research."

"Oh sure, you've sat in a room at the University of Winnipeg reading old documents. No, I'm talking about hardcore research where you wake up every morning wondering if this will be the day you make a discovery, or will it be more hours and hours of wasted time. And then one day you find it. You find that missing piece of the puzzle, and you look down and it's the full picture, and you know in your gut that this is it. This is the one thing that at that specific moment not a single other person in the world knows." She paused and looked Hal directly in the eyes. "I have evidence that shows where he attended university when he disappeared."

"You mean the universities in France, Italy, and Germany?"

"How do you…could you know this?"

"That's where you travelled to over the last two years. Remember, I filled out the travel funding requests because you were too busy."

"Well, sure, you knew where I went, but you didn't know why, so that was just a lucky guess, and you can't tell anyone before I give that presentation. If you do I'm going to totally destroy you."

"Katherine, Katherine, lighten up a little. There's no reason for me to spoil the surprise. This is your research and it sounds fascinating."

"That's more like it."

"I take it you found evidence at all those universities?"

"Yes, well, as I was saying, there were hours and hours of research involved."

"Could you cut to the *Reader's Digest* version?"

"There's evidence in the university records that shows he was there."

"And nobody knew because…?

"He used another name."

Hal just looked at her, knowing that she wanted to tell. At last she leaned forward. "John Falstaff."

Others enjoying their breakfast looked over when Hal jerked upward in his seat with enough force that it sent a teacup to the floor.

"Hal, what is it?"

"But don't you see it? Sir John Falstof was the soldier who opened the Boar's Head in Eastcheap. They took you to Eastcheap. Falstof had a courtyard built for theatre performances next to the Boar's Head tavern. You're telling me that Falstof became William's Falstaff while he was in university and then again when he wrote the plays."

"I'm not following you, Hal."

"He was a writer, so he didn't do anything original. He took names he knew and put them in places he already knew."

"That sort of sounds nice, Hal, but keep in mind that the real Falstof was dead before William was born. Besides, I don't hear you saying anything that would lead to my being kidnapped."

"Then let me ask you one question. Who paid for that European education?"

"It sure wasn't the long dead Falstof."

"Right, but it had to be someone who knew and liked William. For him to use that name there must be a connection to the Boar's Head tavern. But the original tavern burned in the Great Fire."

"So?"

"The tower they wanted to toss you from was built…"

"…as a memorial to the Great Fire of 1666. Yes, Hal, I read the tourist guide books too."

"Was this all just happenstance or some kind of historic symbolism?"

Hal stood up rather excitedly, but quickly retook his seat when he realized Katherine hadn't moved.

"Happenstance, Hal. I don't see any connections between a fire that happened long after William was dead, some other dead guy who owned a bar, and what happened to me yesterday."

"What about this?" Hal laid the lapel pin on the table.

"Interesting. It's cheap metal. You can see where the pin part of it on the back broke. What is it?"

"Someone tried to steal my satchel yesterday when I was looking for you. It came off his coat."

"Some stranger tried to rob you on the street?"

"Well, not on the street. Actually, someone tried to rob me in The Shakespeare up the road a bit."

"The Shakespeare? Wait, isn't that a bar?"

"A pub, well actually half of it is a lounge with soft comfy sofas and chairs; the other half is a restaurant."

"So, your way of trying to find me was to go to a bar. Gosh, I feel so special."

"This from the same woman who went out dancing and drinking with guys she met on the internet?"

"I explained that."

"Well, at least I slept in my own bed."

"Don't you raise your voice to me!"

"Katherine, look at the pin. What do you think that is?"

"Hmmm, it's a poorly designed quill in a circle."

"Yes. A broken quill, just like the name of the group Broken Quill Society who made the magazine. It was their office I went to when I was trying to find you."

"After you went to the bar."

"Fine, after I was at the pub. The person who tried to rob me was in the office clearing it out."

"And you didn't immediately grab him by the neck and hold him for the police? Oh my, sorry, I should have thought before I said that. Maybe you should've threatened him with manly muscle."

"Really funny. Tell me Katherine, what does Prospero do at the end of *The Tempest*?"

"He breaks his staff and then throws it and his book of magic into the sea."

"And what does that mean?"

"It's symbolic of Shakespeare not writing anymore because *The Tempest* was his last play."

"And why do people think that?"

"Stop talking to me like I'm one of your students. We both know that it's because his staff is symbolic of his breaking his pen, crap, his quill. A broken quill. Hal, I can't think of any reason why knowing where Shakespeare went to university is such a problem for other people."

"They think you know something you really don't. It involves Shakespeare, the Boar's Head, and wait a moment, the story in the magazine has something about an iron chest. Do you know anything about a chest?"

"A chest? No, I don't know anything like that."

"How about old bones like the title of the story where it mentions the bones of Shakespeare?"

"No, that's just silly. But, I think you're right. We need to find out who paid for William's education. Mind you, when I did the research I should have run across that, so I don't think we'll find anything."

"We won't if we just look in the same spots. Where was it that you didn't look?"

"Good question. From what you've said, we need to start with the history of the Boar's Head Theatre."

"Agreed."

Katherine pulled pound notes out of her pocketbook while Hal consulted his phone before putting it back in his pocket.

Katherine soon had her own phone in her hand and was talking to someone about getting "permissions at the last moment." Rushing out the door, she stated, "University of London, Special Collections department. But they're only open for a little this morning because the head of the collections is going to the conference in Oxford."

"I have the tube route. On my new app. My students would be proud with how trendy I've become."

Within minutes, the pair stood at the platform at Victoria tube station waiting for their train. Each train brought with it a blast of air pushed in front by the speed the trains reached in the tunnels. Hal fought an urge to cover his ears as each train seemed louder than the one before. Faces in the passing windows were mocking and the indifference of those around became symbolic of nameless hordes of cattle waiting for the slaughter.

The small LED sign overhead indicated their train would arrive in one minute, and the crowd began to swell, pushing Hal towards the yellow safety line on the platform. Katherine, not worried about rules, stepped over the line to ensure she would be first to get on board.

Hal tried to call to her, to remind her not long ago, they saw someone killed by a train, but to no avail. Conversations filled the air as everyone, or so it seemed, was speaking on their mobile phones, trying to be heard over the noise.

Those on their phones were soon joined by a group of rowdier travellers still recovering from the football match the day before. They were taking swigs from open beer cans when a small fight erupted, and the regular passengers moved to keep away from the fighters.

The rush of the air in the tunnel indicated their train was, indeed, on time, when Hal felt someone or something hit him from behind, shoving him forward into Katherine Hal fell to his knees, and Katherine fell off the platform to the tracks a few feet below. Katherine seemed momentarily stunned by the blow.

"Someone's on the track!"

"It's a suicide, stop her!"

"I think he pushed her!"

Hal leaned over the edge of the platform. "Katherine! Stand up! You need to stand up!"

"Get security! Stop him!"

"Why are you holding me?" Hal pulled away from the hands of the crowd for an instant and leaned back over the edge holding his satchel towards her.

Katherine grabbed hold of the satchel and propelled herself from the tracks. Other hands soon reached to pull Katherine to safety just before the train pulled into the spot she had just occupied. A series of cheers went up.

"What the fuck was that! Oh, my, Hal, what was that? Did you push me? Did someone fucking push me? What was that!"

"Katherine, no, hold on. Are you alright? That was a hard fall. Are you sure you're alright?"

Hal jumped as a strong hand gripped his shoulder. "Hold it right there, mate. Are you alright, ma'am?"

"Yes, yes, I'm fine. I think I'm fine, but I was down there, and the train was coming, and I was down there."

"Come with us and we'll have you looked at."

"Alright. I guess that's alright, but I was standing here and then I was down there."

"I understand. You just come with us. Ma'am, do you know this man?"

"Yes," Katherine looked up to see the face of a rather large and muscular security guard. "And don't call me ma'am."

"It looked to me that he tried to push you off the platform in front of that train and kill you, ma'am."

"What? Him? Wait, did you push me, Hal?"

"No, someone pushed me into you."

"So, you did push her then. You both need to come with me." They were led to an office that was only somewhat cleaner than the police station they had been in earlier and found themselves answering many of the same questions.

"So, you two are not in a relationship then, ma'am?"

"I've told you. We work together. I'm his boss. Further, I'm not old enough to be called ma'am, so knock it off."

"But you vacation together?"

"This isn't a vacation. Attending an academic conference in Oxford is not what I'd call a vacation."

"And you, sir, is there any reason why someone would want to harm you?"

"Well, someone tried to hurt Katherine the other day, as I told you."

"Yes, you have. The problem is, we've received the police report. Tell me, Katherine, do you often go drinking with strange men?"

"So, we're back to that, are we? Hal, we need to get out of here and stop wasting time."

"Hold on, you two. We've been checking the CCT feed and there was nobody deliberately pushing you at all. There was a group of footie fans still having a party and when they started to fight, you just got shoved a little."

"Maybe if you security people did your jobs, then there wouldn't be drunks fighting on the platforms at all. Alright then, Hal, I guess you're in the clear this time. Next time, try to keep your balance."

"There's something else." The officer looked at Hal. "These still photos show something interesting. This person wasn't involved in the fight, but he did leave the station without getting on a train. Do either of you recognize him?"

"What is that? It's a hat. All it shows is a hat. Hal, do you know whose hat that is?"

"This doesn't help. There must be more cameras out there that show a face."

"Sorry, Hal, we haven't found any showing a face yet. We have your contact information, and we'll be in touch if we find one. Hal, if we find evidence that you pushed her or even wanted to push her, then we'll want to have a long talk."

"Hal, you're with me, and we're leaving. This is the same nonsense we heard from the police."

Hal dutifully followed Katherine as she led the way back to the platform so they could catch the train.

"You know, Katherine, there've been way too many accidents and robberies. Somebody really does want you dead."

"Thank you so much for reminding me. I never would have thought that after lying on a set of train tracks moments away from being cut in half. Well? Nothing else you want to add?"

"You would have made a sexy corpse."

"What!"

"Nothing. Oh look, here's the train."

Chapter 13

"WHAT'S SO IMPORTANT about ... Karen, is it?"

"Karen May, and let's keep moving."

They were walking through the campus of the University of London, heading towards The Special Collections Department.

"And Karen helped you out?"

"Jesus, Hal, do you ever listen? Karen knows almost every document in this place. Hell, she's been running it since Moses was a baby. This is where I found a letter from Shakespeare to a theatre company asking about a job when he got back. That letter got misfiled and forgotten about until I found it here."

"I thought you said she knows everything here?"

"Almost everything. And she doesn't know what it is, just where it is. Let me do the talking here." Katherine's back was straight and mouth pursed as they walked into the Special Collections entrance. "Karen May, please."

"Yes, ma'am. If you will take a seat, I'll see if she's still here." The voice came from a young freckled clerk who had recently moved to London from a small town in the Cotswolds.

"I don't have time to take a seat. I'm expected, so get her now. And do not call me ma'am."

The poor girl turned red and ran from her desk. Within moments Hal stifled a laugh as a short woman with grey hair in a tight bun emerged. She was the classic librarian from the suit jacket and slacks to the sensible shoes. The best part was that Karen May had exactly the same facial expression as Katherine.

"Dr. Minola, welcome back. I've already found the documents you requested.

"Good."

"Before you and your, um, friend is it?"

"This is Professor Hal Wales."

"Yes then, before you and your young professor look at the documents, I must ask that you…"

"We don't have time for delays."

"Then I suggest you go to the water closet and tidy up. You're not touching anything in my collections with dirt on you like that."

The two followed directions, and Hal was rather surprised to see the grime on his hands and face caused by the incident at the tube station. When he returned to the front desk, he could see Karen May was sitting with the girl working the desk and discussing some problem shown on the computer screen. He used his phone to access the university internet and began searching for The Queen's Men theatre group. He began to breathe carefully as there was a rush of sound becoming audible to him.

*****

"I'M TRYING TO use a private detective to find some information."

"Really, Hal…" the doctor looked up from his notepad. "How is that working out?"

"The things, clothing and blankets were all purchased in England, so there's a good chance I was born there."

"Hal, I can already see you're getting a little emotional. Watch your breathing and use the pills if you have to. Are you sure you want to go looking for her? I'm not sure you're ready."

"I have to find out…I mean I have to know, I just have to."

"What is it that you want to learn, Hal? And don't tell me you want to know your name and find out who you are. I'm not believing that anymore. What is it you really need to know?"

"Why did she leave me to die?"

*****

THERE WERE A COUPLE of web pages that mentioned the theatre group The Queen's Men in passing but gave no details. Hal tried a different idea and searched for images. His hands shook a little as he enlarged the image of a poster on the phone. He looked at the image of the only woman in the cast performing *A Midsummer Night's Dream* that included Bathsheba Savage as Puck. He stared at the picture, grainy from being enlarged too many times, and tried to make out the facial features of the straight nose, full lips, and piercing dark eyes.

"Hal! Dammit Hal, would you wake up."

Hal closed his eyes and committed the image to memory. "Katherine, you are really beginning to…"

"To what?"

He ignored her and looked at Karen. "Let's go."

They were shown into a small room that had an old oak table on which were several small boxes of documents. Each box was labelled with dates and numbers; as a child, Hal had believed they were secret numbers that only librarians understood.

"I believe these were all the documents you asked for. But, given the lateness of the request, anything missing would require more time on another day."

"I've already let you know that you'll be included in a footnote when my paper is published."

"Yes, yes; I'm sure you'll do that. As you must."

Hal was looking at the boxes and trying to ignore how close Karen was standing.

"And how about you, my young professor, are you seeing anything you really want?"

"Hmmm, well it is warm in here. Could we open a window?"

"Oh, what joy. A window he asks. There are no windows in these rooms and, I'm afraid, no air conditioning at all. But I do agree; it is hot."

Hal felt a little embarrassed as she removed her suit jacket, placed it over the back of a chair, and then returned to her earlier position of standing close enough that they were touching.

"Is there anything else, my young, young man, I can help you with, or has your dear Katherine taken care of that?"

"I beg your pardon." Katherine slammed a file on the table.

"Oh, well then, I seem to have touched a nerve. Do shout for me if you need anything. Or better still," she said, putting a slip of paper in Hal's pocket, "just call me."

There was a moment of silence after Karen left the room, and it was Katherine who finally broke it. "If you're finished looking at her bottom, then perhaps we can get to work."

"Fine. Let's start with what you found the last time you were here."

"It's here in this file. But I doubt I missed anything. Here, this one .... oh, for God's sake, let me show you. It's the letter William wrote asking for a job with one of the London theatre companies. He had to use his real name and have a return address, so that helped me start to track where he was for those missing years."

"Could you imagine being the guy who didn't give Shakespeare a job? 'I'm sorry, Mr. Shakespeare, but I'm afraid that your sonnets don't match our requirements at this time as the market is currently flooded with poetry. Good luck in looking elsewhere'." He looked up at the sound and smiled when he realized the strange snorting noise had come from Katherine. "Katherine, this box has information on the Boar's Head tavern and theatre."

"No, those are books that were written in the 1960s by some academic in Scandinavia. I looked at those before and told Karen they were misfiled. I guess she didn't bother listening to me when I told her to get her act together."

"Well, you know my approach to research. Forget what everyone else looks at and find the items that nobody bothers with."

"I know; you've told the story a hundred times about how you once found the evidence that made your book so popular because an author had written some notes on a ripped-up old envelope. And how nobody had noticed because they were too busy looking at formal diaries and documents. That's a nice story, Hal, and I always appreciate when you tell it, but could you try to focus a little here."

"As I was trying to say, this small box appears to be odds and ends from when this collection was made."

"Well, why didn't you say something instead of just standing there? Make some room on the table and spread these papers out. Now, what're you looking for besides the name William Shakespeare or John Falstof?"

"That's rather hard to describe."

"Then enlighten me."

"This isn't a great time to explain."

"Just answer me. I hate it when you dicker around like this."

"Katherine, I make connections. That's all. I read things and hear things and see things that connect like some sort of a spider web. It's my learning style and I've always done it no matter what other people thought. Satisfied? Can we get back to work?"

"Then do it." Katherine sat on a chair and looked at Hal expectedly.

"It's not something I can turn on or off." His eyes scanned the documents and letters spread on the table. "Hold on. I think I do see something. Letters…those two…the same parchment used…different writing…but one matches the handwriting on that one…move the first away…that one is a performance notice…but the year is wrong…that one has the right year…and that piece shows signs of having been bound by stitches…part of a book…saved by this letter writer…connect this … discard those…and that has a clear date and matches this letter…a record of a performance…there…what is it I'm seeing now?"

"Hal, look at this!"

"Names…a list of people watching a performance…why does that matter?"

"Hal, snap out of it!"

"Dammit Katherine, what is it?"

Katherine said nothing. In her hand was Karen May's blazer and there, underneath the lapel, was a small pin comprised of a circle and a broken quill. "Take a look at this. She must be one of them."

"She doesn't seem like the type to plot your murder, though."

"And what type would that be? One with a cute bottom?"

"A cute what? And you say I can't focus."

"At least tell me that you found something in this pile of trash."

"I don't know."

"What do you mean, you don't know? How can you not know? We need to leave before she gets back, so tell me if risking my life was worth it or not."

"Hold on." Hal took out his cell phone and began to take photos of the collection of letters and documents he had moved together.

"Hurry up."

"This phone's camera takes time to focus. Just wait."

Katherine had her hand on the door knob and the second Hal finished, they left the room and headed for the outside door. As they passed the clerk, Katherine snapped her fingers. "Ms. May would like you to clean up the reading room. And be fast about it. Oh, and make sure that the modern books are put on the correct shelf this time. I don't want to see anything misfiled the next time I'm here."

"Yes, ma'am," was the reply, and the clerk scurried away.

"I wish people would stop calling me ma'am. Do I look like a ma'am, seriously, Hal, do I?

"I wish you wouldn't ask me questions like that. You don't need to be so mean when you talk to people."

"If she doesn't want to be talked to like that, then she should present herself differently. Did you notice how tight her blouse was and how short that skirt was? Why am I asking you? You probably committed the scene to memory. You could learn the same lesson."

"Not to wear a short skirt?"

"Pay attention. You show up to teach classes wearing blue jeans and sport shirts. Buy some suits and ties so you look professional."

"Really? That's what you want to talk about now? So, Kate, shall we find the tube station?"

"Do not call me Kate." She was going to add something more, but Hal was looking directly in her eyes.

"Yes, ma'am."

"Oh my, somebody is sleeping on the sofa tonight." There were students on the university pathway with grins. "Yup, he's being a bugger. Nothing for you tonight, matey."

This brought Katherine back to her regular self. "Why are you irritated with me? You were the one checking out Karen's bottom."

More students stopped at that. "Is she talking about Karen May? She must be ninety. Hey, this guy was checking out Karen May."

This only encouraged her to continue. "So, tell me, you apparently young and apparently attractive professor, what's so special about her."

"She's kind and soft spoken and does have a nice bottom, I suppose. But, best of all, she's not you."

At that, the growing crowd of students began to applaud. Katherine turned and walked away.

"Kate. Fine, Katherine, the taxi stand is this way."

Katherine was forced to turn and move back through the students towards Hal; however, her expression was enough to silence students with the warning of what may happen to them if they were ever in her class.

Chapter 14

THE PAIR JUMPED into the back of a black taxi waiting in a line at the front of the main university entrance, forcing the driver to put down his copy of *Learn Croatian in Thirty Days.* "Where to?"

Katherine looked at Hal with a puzzled look. "Well, you're the one who thinks he's in charge. Where are we going to next?"

"Harrods, if you will, driver."

"Harrods it is."

"Harrods? Really, Hal? Somebody wants to kill me and you want to take a break and get a pair of socks?"

"Do you have a better idea?"

"Well, let me think. We're in a city with many, and I mean many, collections of historical documents."

"Such as?"

"Let's start with the collections at the Globe Theatre. I'm sure they have plenty there we can check."

"If there was anything, it would have been found long ago."

"The London Library. The British Library. How about the Women's Library?"

"Harrods."

"What does Harrods have that's so special besides cute ties?"

"There's a vault in the basement where they have a small, but interesting collection of old documents. It's been a while, but I may know someone there who could help."

"I'll trust you on this, but we don't have any time to waste. Hold on a moment." Katherine moved closer to the Plexiglas screen separating the passengers from the driver. "Driver, my friend here says you're driving too slowly."

"Did he now?"

"He says a New York cabbie could drive faster than you."

"Oh, really?"

"I don't believe him. In fact, I have a ten-pound note that says he's wrong."

"Make it twenty."

"Done."

Both Hal and Katherine were pinned to the back of the seat by the acceleration and, as neither had bothered to put on a seat belt, were soon being tossed from side to side. The most interesting part of the journey, mind you, was at a classic roundabout where the driver, who seemed to be having much too much fun, went around the circle three times at the fastest possible speed.

The taxi arrived in front of Harrods and stopped in a zone clearly marked *no standing*. The driver jumped out and opened the back door.

Katherine was the first to emerge and, quickly regaining her composure, nodded her approval at the driver. "Pay the man and do not question his competency again." Emerging, Hal took out his wallet and handed the man the fare and the twenty pounds from the bet, stopped, handed him an extra ten and asked for a receipt because "This is a business expense and it's going on her account anyway."

A few minutes later and Hal had led Katherine to an area in the lowest level of the store.

"Alright then, this is an entire bank with tellers and everything. Nice going, Hal. So, how's this going to help us?"

Hal motioned to a bank manager who, after some hushed whispers, indicated they should follow him. Behind a simple looking door was a narrow hall, which gave way to a larger well-lit room.

"Hal, check out this vault door. It looks ancient."

"There were people back when the store first opened who didn't trust banks, so they came here after learning about a vault that would be impossible to break into. That, and the idea that nobody would ever think about valuables being left in a department store, meant it was once full of treasures. Some of those valuables turned out to be documents. With the passing of time, some items wound up becoming property of the store."

"So, you've been here before?"

"I have an old friend who told me about it and invited me to take a look. And here he is. Jarrod, my dear friend."

Katherine was not sure what impressed her more: Jarrod's height, his lack of body fat or even muscle, or the way he wore a purple satin shirt with lace cuffs and made it look good.

"Harry, come here! Give me a smooch!" The two men exchanged a kiss on the cheek in a flamboyant European tradition. "Oh, love, still carrying that wonderful satchel I gave you. Didn't I tell you it was all you wanted? And who is this lovely creature?"

"Jarrod, I would like you to meet Katherine."

"Katherine, my love, have you looked at Hal's satchel? No? Oh, you just must. I picked this up while I was in Mexico. You have this beautiful Aztec sun hand tooled into the leather. I saw it and just knew who would love it. Isn't it just gorgeous?"

"Yes, I suppose it's nice."

"Speaking of gorgeous, Hal, how do you know this lovely woman?"

"She's my boss?"

"Boss? Nonsense. You're far too young for that title. No, we have to think of a more appropriate title for you."

"Well, I'm the department chair where we teach."

"Oh, that's still not a nice-sounding title. Anyway, before you leave, you simply must come upstairs so we can check that blush you use. You're simply more spring than that autumn you wear."

Before she had a chance to reply, Jarrod had turned away.

"Harry, my love, what is it that Jarrod can do for you? Oh, and please include a makeover at the end of whatever you need. We have some suits that just came in that would be absolutely gorgeous on you. And, yes, I can still get the store discount."

"That's just what I was telling him." Katherine's eyes were wide open. "I told him he needed to dress more professionally in suits and ties."

"And a good pair of black shoes."

"Patent leather of course."

"A red tie."

"And a better haircut."

"Oh yes, a haircut as well. You know Katherine, we should get together and compare notes."

This time it was Hal's turn to interrupt. "If you're finished making me look like a model, we came here for another reason."

"Right, love, you want to see something?"

"I want to see the diaries from, let me think, 1585."

"City?"

"London."

"Right, love, make it easy for a bloke. I may need to get a trolley." Jarrod slipped inside the vault, and Hal took Katherine to another room that was devoid of any furniture but for a single pine table.

"Diaries, Hal?"

"What most people don't seem to realize is London was almost like Nazi Germany back then."

"Sure, I know. People watched everyone else and could make money if they turned in a criminal. You're thinking they wrote about criminals in the diaries, aren't you? Are there diaries from anyone famous in there?"

"All the well-known diaries, those by famous people and such, are in Special Collections where they get read by every graduate student with an idea. Many years ago, somebody with money made their own collection of diaries."

"Do they know who it was and why they did it?"

"Harrods won't say who made the collection. There's a thought the collector may have been trying to keep something from being made public but didn't want to destroy the books."

"Hal, if you're going to tell me some story about the Queen having a bastard son that became William Shakespeare, I'll hit you."

"Don't worry, this isn't Hollywood, and that theory is utter garbage. They won't say who set it up, but when the storage fees are no longer paid, the items become property of the store. They've been available to look at for some time, but nobody knows about them. It's not like the store is going to suddenly say "hey we're taking people's valuables' because someone missed a payment."

"Alright loves, here we are." Jarrod brought a trolley with several boxes through the door. "Good luck to you with this. I have to run, but I'll be back. It seems there's a member of parliament upstairs who can't decide on a gift for his wife, or mistress, or something like that. Anyway, toodles."

"Hal, there must be dozens of diaries in these boxes, and you still haven't told me what we're looking for."

"Think of it. The entire Shakespeare family disappeared overnight. Do you know what they did wrong?"

"We know that there were charges brought against the father for not paying taxes. Even William did business that wasn't exactly legal. There're some researchers in Wales at Aberystwyth University who found William was charged with hoarding grain during a famine and even lent money at a rather high interest rate."

"Back when I was writing about the early days of the Hudson Bay Company…"

"For that book *Follow the Trade; Follow the Poetry.*"

"Right. Anyway, when I was looking at documents at a customs house, I found some old ones showing John Shakespeare was being watched for not paying duties on imports from Europe."

"And you never thought of telling me?"

"I didn't know you at the time."

"You still could have told me when we met the first time."

"Fine. Anyway, I think we should look here."

"Why not the customs house?"

"Because we're nowhere near Ottawa."

"How would it wind up in Ottawa?"

"It was left behind from all of those documents taken to Canada during the war. Can we get started or are you just going to ask me questions for the rest of the day?"

"Just one more, Hal. I know your mind works a little strangely sometimes, but what's the connection between paying duty and a diary?"

"People wrote about what they were up to, and my guess is that there was an inside person being paid off to let John get books through."

"You've seen the diary?"

"No."

"So, instead of trying to find out who wants to kill me, you want to look at 400-year-old diaries and hope to find something?"

"The secret that somebody wants to kill you over may be here."

"So, what are you standing there talking for? Let's get started."

Hal and Katherine took each diary out of a box, checked to see if dates listed corresponded to what they needed and, if the dates worked, began the task of reading handwritten Victorian scribbles. They learned of preparations for weddings and funerals, of teen angst, guilty pleasures, and gossip about people whose bones had long turned to dust.

Katherine sneezed. It was an occupational hazard of reading old books covered in dust. Unfortunately, it wasn't a dainty, ladylike sneeze but one that started with a slight intake of breath, a loud expulsion of air, and a high-pitched sound which could be described as a horse whinnying.

"God bless?"

"Don't be rude, Hal."

She had sneezed frequently while in university libraries tracking down where William Shakespeare was educated. In France, she had earned the nickname of Katy Katchoo. She dabbed a tissue to her nose, remembering those long hours in uncomfortable chairs looking for that one document to prove a theory. Sneezes seldom happen just once, and Katherine always sneezed three times in quick succession. Each of the remaining two was more powerful than the first, with the whinnying becoming even higher pitched.

"If you need to take a break…?"

"It's just an allergy, so never mind."

"I know what you mean. I have an allergy to perfume."

"Are you saying I wear too much perfume?"

"No, you smell just fine."

"How often do you smell me? That's a little strange, don't you think?"

"When did we start talking about this? Are you finding anything?"

"Am I finding anything? Hal, I've spent far longer then you have going through hundreds and hundreds of documents in multiple countries. And you want to know if I've found anything?"

"I was just asking."

"Well, let me ask you something. Do you think if I'd found something I'd still be looking at these things?"

"Well, I was just trying to be nice."

"Instead of trying to be nice and asking stupid questions, just read faster so we can get out of here."

There were a few moments of silence.

"Go ahead, sneeze again."

"Enough of this nonsense, I need to get to Oxford."

"Katherine, we'll go tomorrow. We need to figure this out first."

"Don't you dare tell me what I need to do. The conference started yesterday, and I was supposed to be there from the beginning. Don't you forget that I'm the one invited to speak in Oxford. I'll be the one getting another article published as a result. This is about my career, not yours and I don't need you to hold me back. As for this…" She opened another diary and looked at it disdainfully for a moment, sneezed three times rapidly, and began to read: "Three packages for J. S. from France. Given six shillings. Want more next time. Books are Catholic. Oh, crap! I'm holding the proof right here."

"Catholic?"

"Of course. Given the politics of the time, books by Catholic authors would have been frowned on. It looks like John Shakespeare was bringing in books from Europe, which could've got many people into trouble with the law."

"Is there another entry? There must be more in there."

"Hal, look at this. Several pages have been removed. Not several of them together so you'd notice right away. You know, whoever these people are, they're really beginning to tick off. I mean, trying to kill me is one thing, but defacing a book, especially an old book like this? I'm telling you they should bring back beheading, or maybe public floggings. That's it, deface a book and get flogged by an English professor."

"Let me look at that. Those pages were removed with care. Look at the straight cut and how adjacent pages aren't damaged."

"Great. We need to find a librarian with a scalpel. Let's get out of here."

Hal took out his phone and sent a text. Within a few minutes, Jarrod entered, looking as happy as before. "Find everything you needed, love?"

"Who was here before us? Who wanted to see the diaries?"

The tone in Hal's voice caused Jarrod to stop smiling. "I did hear there was someone in the other day, but I wasn't working…"

"Yes, you were."

"So, I was, but I don't know…"

"Yes, you do. Who was here, Jerry?"

"Just some silly girl. American type, you know, long blonde hair, short but leggy at the same time. Not educated though. She sounded like one of our foster sisters who didn't get through high school."

Katherine was watching and listening with a shocked expression.

"Where is it, Jerry?"

"Where's what?"

"Don't play games, Jerry, I know you too well. The souvenir. The little bauble you couldn't resist."

Jerry dug into a pocket and tossed it to Hal. "It's not worth anything, and you can't tell anyone. I need this job."

Hal looked at an all-too-familiar pin with a broken quill and tossed it back to Jerry.

"I guess it's better than taking from the store. Better hold on to that; it could be worth something one day." He glanced to Katherine: "I need the bathroom. Back in a flash."

On his way, he noticed a security guard in the jewellery department watching two young girls who appeared extremely nervous. Hal smiled as the clerk, on hearing they were trying to buy a present for their stepmother's birthday, announced there was a small discount for paying cash. Even Hal could tell that the girls' pile of coins was not near the asking price.

Hal had an idea and approached the clerk. "Hi, do you do custom jewellery here?"

"Well yes, sir, we certainly do. Are you looking for an engagement and wedding ring set?"

"Oh, no, nothing like that."

"Then how can I help you, sir."

"Well, I have this pin, and I was wondering what you can tell me about it."

"Let's have a look. This is really poor metal and poorly made on top of that. No girl would want this as a present."

"Oh, no, it's not about a girl."

"What is it you need to know, sir?"

"Is there any way you can tell me who made it? I kind of want to find the owner."

"Let me look through my little jewellery loop. There's usually a maker's mark to be found, but you can see that the pin part of it is missing, and the mark would have gone on that section. You do know who the owner is?"

"I really don't know. It's kind of detective work."

"You're a detective?"

"No, I'm an English professor. It's just that sometimes I like to figure out mysteries."

"Oh, I like mysteries too. So, tell me, who do you like better: Hercule Poirot or Miss Marple?"

"I've always been special to Miss Marple, you?"

"Hercule. I could always hear his Belgian accent in my head."

"Many people still think he was French."

"Silly them. I wonder what would have happened if the two had ever got together, for, say, drinks later?"

"Oh, not today, unfortunately, but if you have a number, then we could always meet up on another day."

"I can take a look on the electronic records. Most jewellers take pictures of special orders, you know, in case of theft, so it's easier to track."

"I appreciate that, Veronica." Name tags are often a single man's friend. "I'm Hal, by the way."

"Hal, good to meet you. What I need to do is enter a description. Lapel pin, metal, with a feather?"

"It's a quill. You know, the kind that was used for writing for a long time."

"That's interesting. All done. And the results are…absolutely nothing to be found. You know, this is so poorly made, they probably didn't keep records of it."

"That may be a copy of a better one though. How old are the records?"

"Good question. There's another database for much older jewellery, but it doesn't have any snaps at all. As older records are digitized, they often don't have a sample to photograph, so they just put up a description. Give me a couple moments… and here we are, Hal. Take a look at this."

Hal went around the counter to read the screen "Fifty pins made in 1956. Wow, that was a long time ago. Any mention of who they were made for?"

Veronica checked another page. "This is a copy of the invoice. Paid by BQS. Does that person you're looking for have those initials?"

"Actually, yes."

"He must be old then. It was 1956, after all."

"I'm betting it may be a family thing. You know, passed down over generations."

Hal put Veronica's business card, with her mobile number on it, into his shirt pocket and headed in search of the men's room.

He was smiling and trying to remember the lyrics to the Elvis Costello song *Veronica*. He had already decided this was a phone number he was going to follow up on later. The first washroom was closed for cleaning, but Hal followed a sign that led to what appeared to be an employees' bathroom. It had one door with that strange milky glass over top of it, one stall and one sink, but he went in and locked the door.

"Occupied." He could hear squeaks as something was pushed into the washroom. "I'll be done in a moment if you just want to wait."

Hal stepped out of the stall to find a mop and a bucket with a bottle of toilet cleaner in the mop wringer. The mop beside the bucket looked well used.

"I guess they couldn't wait." Hal washed his hands and before trying to leave. "Hello! Is anyone out there? You locked the door and I can't get out."

Hal turned at the sound of a splash and saw the bottle of toilet cleaner had fallen in the bucket. Hey, a little help! What's that smell? Hey! Somebody! Unlock the door."

The stench from the chemicals was becoming intense, and Hal looked for options. He used the mop to hit the small window over the door. The glass didn't break, but it did crack, and the thudding noise Hal was making brought a security guard who opened the door. "What's going on in here?"

"Someone locked the door and I…"

"What's that smell? You, don't you move."

Hal watched as the security guard grabbed the bucket and, after pouring it into the toilet, flushed. "That'll take care of that. So, why'd you mix ammonia and bleach? Were you trying to hurt yourself?"

"No, I was in the stall and someone pushed the bucket in. I was trying to get out."

"Next time, you should lock the door."

"I did, really, and then when I tried to get out it was locked from the outside."

"Tell, you what. I'll go inside and you can lock the door from this side. Here's the key." Hal locked it as he was told and a moment later the door flew open as the result of one good pull from the guard. "Doesn't seem like much of a problem to me. Do we need to go have a long talk?"

"No, no, I'm fine really. I'm on my way back downstairs. There're people waiting for me and all."

"You be more careful next time and make sure to use the washrooms meant for customers and not staff."

"Of course, the customer washroom next time for sure." Hal hurried away, not wanting to see the inside of yet another security office. "Damn it, did I push or pull?"

He returned to the room in the back just in time to see Jarrod slip a small package into Katherine's hand. Katherine nodded in his direction but addressed Jarrod. "So, is it Jarrod or is it Jerry? And what happened to that posh British accent you had?"

"Oh, love, I don't know what you are talking…" He stopped as the glare directed towards him was enough of a reproach. "Look, lady, it's this way, nobody here is going to hire Jerry from Saskatchewan to help them shop. So, I became Jarrod from Milton Keynes."

"It sounds like you've known Hal for some time. You called him Harry? And what was that about a foster sister?"

"You could say we grew up together."

"Explain."

"Not my place to say."

"It could be my place to mention to Harrods' management that you love, what was the word, souvenirs."

"What the hell? Hal, what the hell is this about?"

"She won't let it go, so just tell her, Jer."

"God, you work for this? Here goes then. We grew up in the system going from foster home to foster home. One night Harry became our Prince Hal."

"How?"

"Shit, lady. Hal?"

"Tell her."

"There's a bunch of kids with the foster parents and everything's fine. Hal and me are both twelve at the time."

"I. It's Hal and I, not Hal and me."

"Seriously, lady? Anyway, early one morning we all wake up to Hal screaming at our foster parents about what they're doing."

"And what was that?"

"Let me be gentle about this; they were having a little morning delight before all the kids woke up. Poor Hal opened their bedroom door and was yelling about stopping him or something like that."

"Oh my, oh my."

"I love the way you snort by the way."

"Just tell me what happened next. How did he become your prince?"

"He calls 911 and the police arrive. They're having a big laugh and the rest of us are still not sure what happened. So, they look in his room and see nothing wrong, and then they look in the foster parents' bedroom and all hell breaks loose. It seems they forgot about something on the nightstand. Oh, I do love the way you snort."

"I can't help it. What was on the nightstand?"

"Cocaine. Before we knew it, there were more cops, and social service ladies were there packing us all up and sending us to other homes. Me and Hal wound up going together. Sorry, sorry. Hal and I."

"And the foster parents?"

"That was something. It turns out they were doing more than a line or two. They were using the older kids in high school to sell the stuff. Last I heard, they were both sent to jail for all sorts of things, you know, drugs, child endangerment, and the like. They didn't charge any of those older teens because the court felt they didn't have much of a choice. He kind of became a hero to us that night. But it's still funny. What else makes you snort like that?"

"Jerry, perhaps you need to back up a little before I smack you silly."

"Oh, stop being a tease."

"If you value your nuts, I'd back away, Jer." Hal was grinning.

"Hal, smarten up! I'm asking him questions."

"Jesus Christ, Hal, you going to just stand there and take this shit from her? Christ, she's worse than Queen Mary."

Katherine stood in front of Jerry. "And who is she?"

"She was a real piece of work. Used to boss him around nonstop, and he just went along with it because a real girl was talking to him. I used to call her Queen Mary. He came in one night and I told him I see Queen Mary has been with you. He was all disoriented because he believed whatever she was saying. I watched him go from being our hero to being turned into a little coward, scared even to disagree when she insisted on telling him what to eat and what to wear."

"What happened to her?"

"One day we're at the house and I'm doing school homework, and in comes Queen Mary. She finds him reading an Agatha Christie novel, and she goes nuts about that being a terrible book. So, he leads her to the door and opens it. As she's leaving, he kicks her in her ass and slams the door. That was the end of her. So, do I have to call you Queen Kathy now?"

Chapter 15

THE TAXI RIDE back to the hotel was uneventful as both closed their eyes, feeling a combination of hunger and fatigue. They stood outside the hotel for a few moments before turning in unison and heading towards Victoria station. On the top floor, they slipped into a small booth in Garfunkel's Restaurant and placed two orders of fish and chips with the server. The food and then the plates disappeared over the next 30 minutes until all that was left was a new pot of tea and two cups.

"Alright, Hal, let's try to put all of this together. I have the proof of where William Shakespeare went to school; however, there's more to this."

"Right. We now know that John Shakespeare was illegally importing books that would have upset people in Elizabethan England."

"Enough to get arrested over."

"Enough that it caused the family to disappear for a stretch."

"So, Hal, who was he importing the books for?"

Hal took out his phone and looked at a few of the pictures he had taken. "There it is."

He pushed it over to Katherine, who looked at the pictures and said "I don't follow, Hal. Where is this from?"

"Sorry. It's one of the records from the Boar's Head Theatre we saw at the university. It lists people and where they were sitting for this performance."

"I'm too damned tired for this. What am I not seeing?"

"There, Katherine…right there."

"Alright. John Shakespeare is written in one of the many spellings of that last name, if it's the same person. You know how hard it is to track one person back then? Most people were illiterate, so a birth record and a marriage licence could have different spellings and that's true of William."

"It's the right person." Hal scrolled to another photo. "This page shows that William is listed as helping with the costumes that day. Both father and son were there. Now, take a look at that first photo and tell me who it says John was sitting beside."

Katherine took a sip of tea before looking down at the phone. She sputtered and used a napkin to cover her mouth. "Is that who I think it is? No, Hal, this could mean…"

"It's the only thing that makes sense."

"Then when we go to Oxford tomorrow…"

"We might be heading into the arms of the Broken Quill Society."

"But what's the secret they're willing to kill over? I can't think of anything like that."

"I think I'll find it tomorrow."

"You mean, WE will find it."

"No, Katherine. I won't let you go. You have to let me take your place."

"You! You want to take MY place! I don't think so. It's my chance to make a name for myself outside of Canada, and I won't let you take that from me."

Hal realized that heads had turned towards the argument, and saw the server approach to place their bill on the table.

"Katherine, I don't want something to happen to you. I can't let that happen."

"Why not? You love me?"

"Ah, no, of course not."

"You want to protect me like I'm a child?"

"Protect, well, yes. But not as a child."

"Or did you look down my blouse this morning after all?"

Hal sat back in the booth and rubbed his temples. Finally, he stood up, tossed a few bills on the table, and took the bill as a receipt before looking directly into Katherine's eyes. "Yes." With that, he turned his back and left while Katherine, much to her surprise, scrambled to keep up with him.

"Katherine, let's change hotels. They won't think of looking for you in another hotel."

"Hal, I'm too tired to think about doing that. We can just ask the front desk for new room cards so nobody can get in."

"Perhaps we can just change rooms and be done with it."

"Alright Hal, if that's what you think is best."

New rooms were not possible that night, but the front desk staff were more than willing to give them new cards.

"Hal, I think we should stay together in your room again. You know, just in case someone does try and break in."

"If you insist; you go in and I'll be right there."

Before the door closed behind Katherine, Hal reappeared holding the bed comforter from her room.

"No reason to get cold lying on the top of the bed this time." He threw the comforter on half of the bed. "Feel free to tuck yourself in tonight."

Katherine went to the washroom to change and came back to find Hal sitting at the desk, his face pale. "I don't see why you're in a mood, Hal. I'm the one who was kidnapped and almost thrown off a tower. I'm the one they wanted under the train, wasn't I? You, well, you're the one who would be blamed. But that's not my fault."

"There's more to this than you know." He took another one of his pills. "I haven't told you everything."

Katherine lowered her voice: "Hal, why do you take those?"

"They help me relax."

"I think I know what those pills are used for. Jerry said something about your imagination getting away from you sometimes. Is that what's happening here?"

"There are times when reality and fiction seem to blend a little. These are supposed to make the distinction clear. You have to admit, the past couple days have been nuts."

"Yes, they have." Katherine lowered her voice to a whisper. "What is it that you haven't told me?"

Hal reached into the desk drawer, ignoring the photographs and the hand-drawn pictures. Instead, he took out the small lock of red hair and handed to Katherine. "Do you have any idea who could have cut your hair without your knowing?"

"This is just like the story again, isn't it? Before you kill me, you cut a lock of my hair to keep with you."

"The thing is, I don't know how I got it. I found in my wallet. This isn't my fiction, is it? I want to protect you from these people, Katherine. I'm not one of them, believe me."

"I believe you, Hal."

A few minutes of silence elapsed.

"It all started with that story. I haven't taken one of those pills for months, and then that thing shows up in the mail and it's all I can think about. Look, you know me. I've never hurt anyone and you can check. Whatever this is, it isn't me behind it."

Katherine examined the hair. "You didn't make this lock, Hal. You couldn't have."

"Are you sure?"

"Without question. You were out of town that weekend. If I remember, you were up in Edmonton for a meeting with the Alberta Writers Guild."

"What happened that weekend?"

"I got my hair done. You know: coloured and cut. I looked at it the next morning and didn't like what I saw, so I went back to the salon and made them redo it. For free, of course. This is what the colour looked like the first time, so it must have been taken from the hair they trimmed. It was only this shade for a few hours. Don't worry, you haven't been cutting my hair in your sleep or anything like that."

"Who would have access to your hair trimmings, then?"

"I don't know. Just the girls at the salon I suppose. Hal, if someone is trying to set you up, then this is more evidence that could be used against you. I don't think either one of us imagined that idiot trying to run us off the road in Calgary. I went with someone to talk about my research only to wake up at the top of a tower. No, Hal, this is real. It's not your imagination."

He looked at the desk.

"Hal, do you hear me? You're not one of them, and this is not fiction; this is somebody else's doing."

"That does make me feel better, I guess. I'm a little confused about one thing though. What do you mean you have your hair coloured?"

"You don't think this is my real colour, do you? I mean, I'm a redhead, but not this colour. Didn't you notice it changes shades from time to time?"

"No. I always thought it was perfect. That lock of hair, though, means people are getting so close they can put things in my wallet. That's something to worry about."

"Get under the comforter and go to sleep, Hal. Tomorrow, we'll head to Oxford and this thing is going to get settled one way or another."

Chapter 16

"LOOK, DOC, I MEAN, it's been a slice and all, but I need to get a little packing done."

"I know you want to go to London. I just think you're not ready."

"The pills work. I haven't had a major episode in some time, and I want to check a hospital while I'm there."

"Yes, I know."

"What then?"

"Hal, sit down, will you?"

"I just want to look out the window. I guess I'm a little impatient to get moving. Fine, I'll sit."

"I want to go over the women in your life over the years."

"Why?"

"To make a point, Hal. Stop fidgeting and listen. First there was your mother."

"Right. Abandonment issues. And she left me but didn't try to kill me."

"Then there was Jane."

"I know. She killed herself, and I found her and then blocked it out. We covered that."

"The mother figure in that one group home."

"Doc, she was just using kids to sell drugs and I wasn't one of them."

"Yes, but you trusted her, and she let you down."

"I guess."

"Then we have Katherine."

"Oh, hell no; she's not a sister or mother figure, so it's not the same thing."

"But she could be someone special."

"Doubt it."

"You write the stories, even if it's during an episode, and what happens, good or bad, is a reflection of your subconscious."

"Not true."

"You need to acknowledge this. You alternate between wanting to screw her and wanting to kill her."

"No."

"Then Hal, why are you sitting in the corner trying to wipe something off your hands?"

*****

THE PHONE'S ALARM began to chirp, indicating it was time for them to wake. Hal opened his eyes to find himself sitting in a corner, Katherine watching him.

"Were you sitting there watching me sleep?"

"No, I, well…"

"What is with you and watching people sleep? I need the shower, and then we'll get moving."

He was drying when Katherine started talking to him through the door. "I don't want any nonsense from you today, Hal. We have too many things to figure out."

He opened the door and walked into the room, holding the damp towel in front of himself. "You don't want any nonsense from me?" He walked to the desk and found the copy of *Terrific Crime*. "Here we are."

"Hal, put some clothes on."

"First, let me read part of the story…where is it…ah, here we are."

Her heart was beating as she looked into the mirror. She took bright red lipstick and applied a generous amount to her full, pouty lips. Her hands began to tremble as she undid buttons on her blouse so her freckled breasts were partly exposed.

When she returned to the bed, Hal took her trembling for fear.

"Sit here," was all he needed to say, and she complied, making sure she was close enough their thighs were touching.

"Hal, I'm so scared by these people that want to kill me. I don't know what I would do if you weren't here."

"Don't worry, Katherine; no one will hurt you as long as I'm around."

Katherine leaned towards him, letting her blouse open slightly. Hal put his arm around her and let it slide down until his hand was on her breast.

"Hal, would you..."

"Hush, Katherine." He kissed her and enjoyed the taste of her lipstick.

"Oh, for God's sake Hal! Stop reading that trash."

"Correct me if I'm wrong, but those buttons on your blouse yesterday didn't undo themselves, did they?"

"That's stupid, Hal."

"You say that, but I see a little blush of the truth." He turned to go back to the bathroom and threw the towel on the floor.

"At least cover your bottom."

"It's called an ass." He turned around and looked at her before closing the bathroom door. "And consider getting some new lipstick."

*****

"IS THIS SUITABLE?" They were both ready and Katherine had her hand on the doorknob. "Would you like me to put on a thick sweater, an overcoat, maybe a nun's habit?"

"What I'd like is breakfast, and we're running out of time."

They headed out of the hotel and towards Victoria station.

"Hold on, Katherine." He stopped at a small kiosk. "Give me a regular tea and one of those tall dark roast blends with two sugars. And a couple of banana muffins, while you're at it."

"We need to eat on the run, Hal. Where do we pick up the bus?"

"That's easy. They put these coloured lines on the floor to help out people who don't know the area."

"Oh, I see. You walk on these and it takes you to the right exit. That's neat."

"Yup. And we just need to follow the one that says bus station."

The line took them to an exit on the other side of the station, where it was simply a matter of crossing the street and walking to the end of the block to find the bus stop where the Oxford Tube bus line picked up passengers.

"There're sure not many people around." Katherine was trying to drink hot coffee quickly, as the driver had made it clear that the no food and drink rule was firmly enforced on his bus.

"Nope." Hal had given up trying to down a hot tea and tossed it a nearby garbage can. "Too early yet. Office workers don't need to be here on a Saturday, and the shoppers haven't shown up."

"Good for us."

"Oh, we'll pick up more. There's something like three stops before we get out of the city."

Most of the handful of the passengers waiting with them made their way to the top of the double-decker bus. Some, like Hal and Katherine, stayed on the first level. By the time the bus had made several stops in the city, even the bottom section was full of friends and strangers in conversations. Both Hal and Katherine caught the drift of two people sitting to their left.

"So far, I've published twelve books and edited several others in multiple genres. It is surprising how many people do not know how to use a contraction or even where the Oxford comma goes."

"Oh my, you must make a great deal of money?"

Katherine elbowed Hal to make sure he paid attention to the elderly woman, professionally dressed, and a younger man in shorts and sandals who was excitedly explaining his life as a writer.

"Yes, but what I really love is the satisfaction of knowing thousands of people have read my work. For me, it's about entertaining and informing the public. There's nothing better than being invited to do a personal appearance in a bookstore or a library and seeing all those smiling faces just waiting for me to start reading. The money, and there is, I will admit, a fair amount rolling in, is just secondary to the love I feel from readers."

"You're like another J. K. Rowling then, aren't you?"

"Well, I do not mean to brag, but we often meet when I'm in Europe to have tea and talk about the projects we're working on."

Katherine was trying to cover her mouth to snifle the snorting; Hal squeezed his knee in an effort not to laugh.

"Oh, that must be wonderful. Tell me some of the titles of your books, so I can pick them up in the bookstores when I get home."

"Tell you what, give me your email address, and I will send you some of the links. I don't always use traditional stores because of the percentage they take off the top. No, as I was telling J, sometimes you have to self-publish and only have electronic books for sale because that's where the money is. I even wrote a book about how to write and publish an e-book, and there is not another book like that out there anywhere."

"Honestly, I don't like those electronic book readers. I tried to use one once, and it was just too hard on my eyes. Besides, I like to lie back in the tub and read a good old-fashioned paperback novel without worrying about dropping it in the water and electrocuting myself. What do you have as a paper book?"

"Well, as I was saying, the bookstores take too much off the top to make the printed books really worth my time. You know, there are some newer types and models of e-readers that I think you might like, and then you can download all sorts of my books."

"So, you don't really have a book printed on paper? Well, then, oh look, a cow."

It was clear that the conversation was over.

"Tell me, Hal," Katherine leaned close as if very serious. "What was your last royalty cheque?"

"I believe it was $14.65. You?"

"Not much more than that, I can tell you. Did you see what she was reading?"

"No."

"It was a copy of *Publishers Weekly*, so she must work in a bookstore or something like that."

"Or she works for a publisher. Now that would be funny."

The bus made a quick stop at a park-and-ride just off the highway to pick up the last traveller heading to Oxford.

"Hal, do you feel like anyone's watching us?"

"No. Nobody's watching us."

"They're waiting for us, then."

"Yes, and there's nothing we can do about that. I take it you're ready to speak at the conference, no matter what."

"You bet. All by memory, as usual."

"That's gutsy. I've seen people try it and fall flat on their face. Is it a 20-minute time limit?"

"Fifteen preferred, but you can speak for twenty. And then they take the questions as always."

"You'll have to speak up if it's outside."

"Hal, do you really think I'll ever have trouble being loud enough? You forget how big some of those old lecture halls we teach in are."

"True enough." Katherine silently rehearsed the presentation again. Her watch indicated they were halfway through the 100-minute trip.

"Katherine, I have to say it again. I think you should let me take your place."

"And I have to say it right back to you, no. Hal, you don't need to worry. Remember, I took care of those guys at the tower. I can look after myself."

"I'm not going to be far away though. You know, just in case."

"You can stick close. I'd like that."

Chapter 17

FIFTY MINUTES LATER, the driver began to call out the stops as they drove into Oxford. They were in the bus aisle, part of the large group getting off at the High Street stop, when they heard the comment, "I will have a story in a journal called *Terrific Crime* soon. It is all about a vampire who becomes part of the worldwide zombie apocalypse." The speaker was the same writer they had listened to earlier, who was now trying to impress a lady his own age. Hal and Katherine had no choice but to watch as he exited the bus while they had to wait their turn.

"Hal, I didn't see which way he went, did you?"

"No, wait, I think I see him way ahead this way."

They tried to run down High Street, but there were already crowds of shoppers mixing with those coming to, or going towards, one of the many churches in the area. They were forced to slow down, so when they reached the intersection of High Street and Corn Market Street, their quarry was nowhere to be seen.

"That's it. I don't see him anywhere. Do you have any idea where he went?"

Hal turned in a full circle. "Yes."

"Where is he? Do you see him?"

"No, I don't see him. Ask yourself, where would any writer go to first and last in any town they travel to?"

"Where what? Wait a minute…I follow what you're talking about…he's got to be over… there."

Together, they crossed the street and entered the local Waterstones Bookstore.

Before they heard him, they saw the store manager rolling her eyes in response to his request. "I know you normally do not do that sort of thing, but I do not see what the problem would be with an electronically published author doing a book signing in the store. I am just the same as any other author."

The manager was trying to motion to one of the clerks to help save her from the situation, but they were having too much fun watching to intervene. "And what would you sign? Their e-readers? Their phones? Look, you need to contact the head office, so just take this business card and email them. Don't phone them because they won't take a call about this sort of thing. Now, if you'll excuse me, I think I hear a delivery at the back door." She hurried away before he could say anything more.

Katherine reached him first. "Hi, I thought I heard you on the bus about being published in *Terrific Crime*?"

"Oh, yes I am, but I've got multiple books out. My name's Dougie, just Dougie. It is like Madonna but for books instead of music."

"Alright then, Dougie, let's talk about that journal."

"Here, let me give you one of my cards. It has my email address, phone numbers, my blog…"

"That's nice, but about the journal…"

"It also has my Facebook page, and how to find me on…"

"Hal, would you talk to this guy before I lose it?"

"No problem. Dougie, listen up. There's a sign over there that says no soliciting, so if you keep it up someone here is going to call the local authorities and you can try to sell a judge one of your books."

"Well, I guess you have my full attention now, but you didn't have to be rude, you know. I have a book that discusses proper behaviour when talking to people. You would be surprised how many business people need to learn…"

"We just have a couple of questions. Are you published in *Terrific Crime*?"

"Yes. It's a wonderful cross genre short story featuring a gorgeous lesbian vampire as a protagonist who must fight for her life after a government conspiracy results in a zombie apocalypse. It is totally original."

"I'm sure I've never heard of another story like it. Really. But that's not what I care about. How do you get in touch with them?"

"That is a good question. I saw they set up an office in London, so I dropped my manuscript off, and they said they wanted it. I've been trying to go back and talk to them, but the office always seems to be closed, and they do not answer calls or emails or anything."

"Who did you deal with?"

"Just this young secretary. She had to be new because I had to explain all sorts of things to her. Do you know what's going on? I want to be paid, and that secretary said that in a few days the journal was going to be worth big money, and everyone would want a copy."

"Do you know any other way to contact them?"

"Look, I just told you I cannot get anyone to call me back. By the way, if you check out my blog, you'll get full details on how to download my latest novel. Some say the cover makes it looks like erotica, and there is a love scene in it that…"

"Let's go, Katherine; he knows as little as we do."

The pair returned to High Street on their way to Catte Street, a narrow side street that looks like the start of an alleyway to nothing rather than a critical short cut for students and academics. They walked between The Radcliff Camera Library and All Souls College as the street widened slightly and the side entrance to the Bodleian Library appeared.

Catte Street was full of people. Men wearing ill-fitting suits or corduroy pants and sports coats mingled with women trying to find the balance between femininity and professionalism, and failing in both respects. These were the visiting academics brought together from different areas of the world for the possibility of being noticed for their expertise and research. Groups formed based on their views about William Shakespeare. One group of bespectacled professors stood their ground when proclaiming it was one man who wrote the plays. A collection of blue jean clad professors believed Shakespeare was a group of writers using a poor actor as the face of their work. Feminist scholars, not to be silenced, interjected at any given opportunity that the fact the plays contain dialogue was proof William was female, as men did not know how to have a conversation, let alone write one.

"Here we go, Hal. Thomas Bodley's pride and joy."

"And perhaps the centre of the society."

"If you're right, that is."

"Do you doubt it?"

"Nope. It sure looks like Thomas Bodely sat beside John Shakespeare at that play."

"Gird your skirt and let's go in."

"What?"

"Follow me."

"No thanks. I've seen enough of your ass for one day."

The duo passed through an entryway where the ticket booth was managed by a smiling middle-aged woman who watched as they made their way to the quadrangle. Just to the left was the entrance to the bookstore, and in front of that there was a small table where conference delegates could pick up their name tags and conference brochures.

Hal smiled at the young lady in charge of the booth. "Good morning. Hal and Katherine from Canada. I see our name tags are right there."

"Well, of course they are. The conference has been running for two days, and you're just showing up now? Were the other presentations not of any interest to you, or do you only come to a conference to hear yourself speak?"

"I'm sorry? You're being rather rude, I must say."

"Well, you're from Canada, so I'll wait for the apology."

Katherine made to push her way in front of him, but Hal politely stopped her. "I've got this one."

He put his satchel down on the table, forcing the young lady to move her tea, and examined the fingernails on his right hand. "I'm guessing you're a graduate student. Magdalen College?"

"Yes."

"Last year of studies, I bet. Finished, what do they call it here? Ah, yes! Finished the writing up and all set to defend your doctoral thesis soon?"

"Next week."

"Fine. But you're more than a volunteer, aren't you? You gave a presentation about your own work, when, yesterday? No, right at the beginning of the conference when half the people weren't here yet, and the others weren't ready to listen?"

"I asked them to be quiet."

"You asked a bunch of university professors to be quiet? My, my."

"They were being rude."

"I'm going to guess that it didn't go all that successfully after you did that."

"Take your name tags and go so I can cross you off my list."

"Jobs are limited in academia and, as you well know, having contacts is important, so are you sure you want to keep up the attitude?"

"The name tag reads Red Deer College. I've never even heard of it."

"Perhaps then, there are some names you will recognize…" With that Hal began to list the names of department chairs, deans, and even university chancellors, implying they would take his phone call in an instant. In reality, he only knew two of them. When he finished, a few people within earshot applauded.

Katherine was beaming. "I didn't know you had that side to you. Well done."

"What can I say? I had a good teacher."

"Thank you."

"It wasn't a compliment."

They took the name tags and walked away.

"Hal, do you think we're being watched now that we're here?"

"You're beginning to think like me, then. Look at the flow of how people are walking. Start to look for the pattern as they come and go from entrances and change who is in the groups. A crowd like this is alive."

Katherine watched, and for a moment saw the motion, except for one person who didn't fit in with the others. "There, over there."

"I see him."

As the crowd moved again, they lost sight of the voyeur.

"Hal, how many do you think there are?"

"Three, that we know of."

"Wait, there were the two that snatched me, and how many did you see? Don't forget about Ms. May."

"I've been thinking about that. I could swear that Davey from Dallas was wearing stage makeup and a phony beard. He could have been one of the men you went dancing with."

"Excuse me?"

"Sorry. One the men who kidnapped you. The fellow I met at the society office in London sounds like the other one you went with."

"That's only two."

"There was also the young woman Jarrod talked to who must have taken those pages. Trust me, Jarrod is specific when he talks about women. But it might be the same girl Dougie was talking about. There's no way Ms. May fits either description."

"Then why did she have the pin?"

"That's something we have to figure out soon."

"By the way, how do you know Davey was from Dallas? Was it his accent, because you really don't get it right when you tell people where you think they're from."

"What do you mean? I'm pretty good at it. I took that linguistics class one semester."

"You think everyone one is from Texas or Mexico. I'll prove it. Where do you think I grew up?"

"Amarillo?"

"Toronto, Hal, Toronto. So I doubt that Davey is really from Dallas. You wait here for a moment or two. I need to check in with the organizers and make sure everything is ready for me to give the key note address tonight."

Katherine saw the person she needed to talk to and ran across the quadrangle to meet her, leaving Hal by himself.

"Watch yourself." a workman got Hal's attention. "We need to set up these chairs. Put 'em up every morning; take 'em down every night as it goes. You may want to stand aside for a bit."

Hal moved out of the way of the workmen and, as there is not much room in the quadrangle, headed into the Divinity School. He loved the building and how its vaulted ceiling was crisscrossed by carved ribs of stone. The large room was full of costumes and props, which took Hal by surprise.

"Excuse me, sorry." He caught the attention of a bespectacled older man with a clipboard. "Could you tell what all this is for?"

"Are you in for the conference?"

"Yes, just got here."

"Oh, you don't know then. The theatre company I'm with is putting on a special production of *Henry IV* tonight. You're welcome to check out everything here. Just don't steal anything."

"Oh, be nice now. Academics don't steal."

"They don't? That's not what I've seen."

"No, it's just that sometimes we borrow things and sort of forget to return them for a few years. Say, I like these costumes. I take it they've contemporized the play a little?"

"They have. It's set in the Second World War. Personally, I would rather they left that alone and did it the way Shakespeare wrote it. What do you think?"

"I can tolerate the modern settings as long as they don't mess with the language. It ticks me off when I hear actors messing with the lines like that. Are there any famous actors I might know?"

"Check that box there. It has the playbills for the performance."

Within moments, Hal was running out the door looking for Katherine.

"Hey, those things cost two pounds each. Damn academics. Borrowed, my butt." He spoke to air as Hal was already gone.

"Katherine, hold up."

"Oh, Hal, I would like you to meet…"

"Look at this playbill. The face right there…"

"Hal, this is the head librarian for the Bodleian Library, Dr. Josie Thomas, the first American to ever earn that title, so please be nice."

"Of course, sorry, I'm so pleased to meet you."

Josie just smiled.

"Katherine, look at this."

"I don't recognize that person, Hal. As I was trying to say, we have permission to look at…"

"It's Davey from Dallas."

"What, why…"

"He's an actor in the play that's being performed here tonight. His real name is Claude Wargrave. He's here."

"Alright then. Try to control yourself. We have permission to look at a collection privately."

Josie looked suspiciously at Hal before addressing Katherine. "I really don't understand the rush to see this collection. You have the keynote address ready, Dr. Minola? Do you not?"

"No, we, I mean I do. However, we have acquired some even newer information that we may be able to prove."

"Very well, you just need to come over here, and we'll go in this room. We were in the process of making a special collection of the effects of Sir Thomas Bodley and were going to put them on display, but there have been a couple of attempted break-ins, so I decided to keep them locked up and not display them for the time being."

"Break-ins? But the books are all safe, right?"

"Oh, yes, Katherine, they are. I even had security doors installed very recently. They lock automatically, and you need a special code to open them."

Hal had time to catch his breath, and before Josie Parker left asked a question: "What did Bodley think of William Shakespeare?"

"Seriously? Thomas Bodley hated theatre. You should know that."

Left alone, Katherine looked to Hal. "Show me that picture again."

"Here. See, right there."

"I guess it could be him. But the guy I saw had a beard, and you said Davey had one, too."

"Sure, a phoney beard. Think about it; he's an actor."

"And when does the play happen?"

"Tonight. Right after your keynote speech."

Katherine let out an audible sigh. "He's here, then."

"They all are."

"Alright then. In the meantime, let's check out this collection. She said it was in this room. Apparently, some of these things were in a forgotten storage cabinet for many years. You have to wonder how that would happen."

"They were probably just misfiled."

"Hal, there's not that much here. Some books, but none of your diaries. Hold on. I know that author. He was Catholic. And it was printed in France."

"Maybe that's one of those missing links, if you will."

"You're right. It was Thomas Bodley sitting beside John Shakespeare at the Boar's Head. I wonder if this is a book given to him there?"

"I don't think he could fit volumes this large under his cloak. He would've received the books some other way, but could've paid John there."

"Alright Hal, what's here that people were trying to break in and find? I mean, it seems that they've been ahead of us half the time, so it must be those quill people."

Katherine began to thumb through some of the older volumes of records pertaining to the library, some detailing what Thomas Bodley had done to increase the collection. Hal was more interested in a small box containing empty ink bottles.

"These are simple gorgeous." He was whispering, but it didn't matter. Katherine was too engrossed in what she was looking at to notice. "I love the way these bottles have turned green with age. I bet Bodley filled up a fancy inkwell using these. And what are these? Glass dip pens? They're Victorian era, not Elizabethan, so they've been misfiled by someone. There's nothing that special here after all, just odds and ends. No wonder it was thrown together and forgotten."

Both of them were moving through the items, looking increasingly disappointed with every passing minute.

Hal picked up another small wooden box. "This is pretty rough. Just slats tacked together. You know, I bet this stuff was meant for the garbage and for some reason didn't make it." He looked through the odds and ends in the box. Hal moved another small bottle aside and noticed something wedged between the slats at the bottom of the box. He used one of the glass dip pens to pry it loose until he could hold it.

"Hal, I think I have something here."

"So do I."

"Hal, pay attention. You know about the black iron chest that Bodley had made to hold cash and valuables?"

"Of course. It was kind of a safe with, what was it, three separate locks so three people had to be present to open it."

"And it was ornate on the outside and far too heavy to be carried away easily."

"Right. It's used for people to put donations into at the Divinity School."

"So, Hal, why is there a listing of a second chest?"

"What second chest?"

"It says in this ledger that Thomas Bodley took possession of a plain chest made of iron with a three-key locking system. I've never heard of that one." Katherine looked like she was going to faint and Hal rushed to her side. "Shit, Hal. The chest. They kept asking me about a chest."

"I know, Katherine. There's one in that story as well."

"Shit. Shit. Shit. There is one."

"Does it say where he put it?"

Katherine recovered and looked at the document. "No, there's nothing like that. It only says it was delivered. They believe it's here; the question is where?"

"I wouldn't have a clue where to start."

"Not a clue here, either."

"Maybe we're thinking about this all wrong."

"What do you have in mind?"

"We're asking where he put it. I think the real question is, what would he put in it?"

Hal looked at Katherine as her eyes grew wide. "Katherine, I bet we're thinking the same thing. Take a look at what I found here."

The noise of the hinges alerted them to the door opening, and Hal slipped his discovery into his satchel.

The young woman who entered was facing outside as she entered to make sure nobody noticed her. Closing the door, she paused momentarily to let her eyes adjust to the light and then began to rummage through the items on the table. Katherine and Hal didn't move, but when the woman moved a couple of steps towards Katherine, it was Katherine who reacted first. Her left fist connected with the right eye of the young lady with enough force to send her head backwards; she collapsed into a distorted pile of limbs on the floor.

"Katherine! What's wrong with you?"

"You saw the way she snuck in. She has to be one of them."

"You don't know that. I'll go get security and get her some help."

"Just wait a minute. I want to talk to her first."

They managed to move the woman to a sitting position and Katherine used a couple of well placed slaps to the face to bring her back to consciousness.

"Why are you slapping her? She could've been looking for a bathroom."

"You're way too trusting."

The woman began to stir and opened her eyes.

"Let's start with the basics. Name?"

"I ain't tellin' you nuthin!"

"Would you like your other eye darkened to match the first? Name?"

"Get away from me!"

"Any more doubts, Hal? She's one of them for sure."

Katherine was moving to a position so she could make good on her threat when Hal stopped her. "Let me talk to her."

"Alright then, but she better talk fast."

Hal bent down and spoke quietly. "I can tell by the way you talk you don't have much of an education and by your accent that you are from, let me guess, Mississippi?

"Decatur."

"And what's your name?"

"Zoe. You're not gonna let her hit me again, are ya?"

"Of course not. There we are. So, when did you team up with the others? I know one's an actor, and I bet he's the one you're with."

"Yessir. We met when he did a play at the theatre back home."

"Nothing wrong with that. So, tell me, what were you looking for in here?"

"A box."

"A box? I bet it's a heavy metal box. That right?"

"Yessir. Have you seen it?"

"What does your friend think is in the box?"

"Don't know. He won't tell me, but I think he might know. Says it's worth a crapload. That's what he said, a crapload."

Hal looked up at Katherine. "Money. Enough to kill over. That's what it's all about then."

Katherine looked rather disgusted. "Let's bring in security and have them call the police."

Zoe launched herself from her seated position with enough strength to knock Katherine off balance. Hal reached out but his hands only brushed Zoe's shoulder.

"Grab her, Hal!"

The door was flung open, and Zoe disappeared into the crowd.

"Which way did she go?"

Hal tried to block the sun with his hand. "I don't see anything."

"There! The door behind the Earl of Pembroke statue."

The chairs in the quadrangle were occupied as the first presentations of the day were underway. Entering the same door as Zoe, they realized they were in the main entry to the oldest section of the Bodleian, the Duke Humfrey Library, and security was already gathering.

"Hold on, you two. Someone just jumped the security barrier, and until we get her, we're closing the doors."

Katherine didn't hesitate but jumped the same barrier. Hal wasn't as lucky, as a large set of hands turned him around and helped him exit the building. Before the doors were closed and locked, he did hear one snippet: "Looks like they went down, not up."

"Down?" Hal spoke out loud. "She was in a basement in that story. That's where she was killed."

Chapter 18

HAL RAN TO THE Divinity School, looking at the weapons on the storage racks for the play that night. He selected a sword, and ran the short distance to the Radcliff Camera, a round library that had started life as an observatory, jumping the barrier. "Move it! Get out of the way!"

"Sir, you can't go down there! Someone call security! We've got a crazy man with a sword heading to the lower floor!"

Many years before, a tunnel had been built between the Radcliff Camera and the Oxford Bodleian. In 2012, it had undergone yet another renovation. Railway tracks had been installed to allow dirt to be excavated when the original tunnel was built. Those same tracks now allowed for a small train to be used to move books to the higher floors of the library. Hal followed the tracks. The overhead lights went out.

"Oh, crap."

A moment later the emergency lights and fire alarm came on.

"Fire? A fire?" He kept running and, fortunately, kept his hands in front of him so when he ran into the door, he didn't hit face first.

"What the hell? What kind of door is this?" In the dim flashing emergency lights, the two sliding doors appeared to be something from science fiction movies. Most of each door was a new type of clear polymer, which could prevent the spread of a fire. The polymer was set in a heat resistant metal meant to prevent anyone from opening them if they were intent on robbery. Just to the right of the doors, he found the keypad used for unlocking the doors.

"It's the four-number keypad, like Josie said. Think it through; what four-digit number would fit? It has to be something to do with the library. After Bodley took over, it reopened in 1602. Wrong. Josie said it was three tries and then you're locked out. What else? Bodley died in 1616. Wrong again."

There was a noise behind him, and it became clear security was heading his way.

"The doors are new, and Josie said she helped program a couple of locks. That's it! It's about her. Let's see what I know about her. She's a woman in charge of a library, but that's no help. She's also American and that's not normal here either. Hold on. Would she pick that here in England? So, what is it?"

Hal rooted around in his satchel until he found what he wanted at the bottom. Hal held up the cheap ring he had won at the ring toss game at the Stampede. "It's just too small. July 4th what?"

His hand flew to the keypad and hit 1776. The doors opened, and Hal stepped through and hit the close and lock buttons just before three security guards reached the door. "Hey guys, do you know the code? Guess not."

In that section of the Bodleian basement were rows of the stacks, the shelving containing books, which went from floor to ceiling. There was shouting down one of the aisles in the stacksand Hal pressed himself against the wall to avoid detection while listening to the conversation of security guards who had come down a different stairwell.

"I saw something down that direction."

"They're calling us back."

"Let me just check."

"No. There's a fire. Everyone needs to help."

Once the guards left, Hal went in the direction they had been and heard a faint cry behind a door. Entering, he found almost complete darkness, the only illumination from the emergency light coming through the now open door. Hal walked around a desk covered with the statistics that a librarian was compiling about books and documents that had frequently been requested in the last quarter. He heard the cry again and turned quickly to see the source: an antiquarian radiator.

"That's it! I just can't take this shit anymore! She's kidnapped and then she's not kidnapped. I follow clues that aren't even clues. I run down here to find there's nothing here at all. I've just had it!"

He picked a large dictionary from the desk and slammed it to the floor. "Well, that didn't sound right." He stomped on the floor a couple of times. "This should all be concrete flooring down here, but that sounds like wood. Unless there's another room under me."

On one wall was a newer built-in shelving unit; another unit clearly had the hallway on the other side. The third had smaller shelves holding books near the top and the radiator attached to the wall near the floor. There was only one wall with nothing on it or positioned before it. Hal ran his hands over it, attempting to find any indication of hinges or a doorknob, but found nothing. Hal turned and looked at the books on the older shelving, trying to make out the titles. "What's here? Everything Edgar Allan Poe wrote, *The Strange Case of Dr. Jekyll and Mr. Hyde*, *Dracula*, *Frankenstein*."

He had to squint in the dim light to see all the titles until one stood out. "Look at that. A copy of Hemingway's *The Sun Also Rises*. Is this the sun in the darkness?" He pushed the book, and then tried pulling it. Finally, he took the book off the shelf. There was no secret system to open a door. Hal removed the other books to make sure.

The wall heater began to moan again, and as Hal was leaving, he grabbed a small knob to turn it off, but found it stuck. He grasped the knob harder, but instead of finding that it turned, he found that he could pull it. As he pulled, the small section of wall it rested on opened and created an opening just big enough to crawl into.

Hal stuck his head in the opening. He had to crouch and slide into the darkness before finding just enough room to stand on the other side of the wall. The noise from the radiator combined with the darkness to become the familiar warning of the onset of another blackout. Hal bit the inside of his cheek and let the pain tell him that this was real, and he was still in control.

He slid one foot ahead, stretching out an arm. There was a dropoff a couple of feet in front, followed by another. He placed a hand to one side and found a cold brick wall which disappeared as he moved down a spiral staircase. As he descended further, a small room began to emerge from the darkness. The 40-watt bulb on a cord hanging from the ceiling provided little light. He could see a card table and folding chairs set up in the middle of the room. The corners were mostly in darkness; however, a moving shape in one corner caught his attention.

"Katherine, there you are. Why are you sitting like that?" All he heard was a muffled response. "A gag? Are you gagged?" He hesitated before finishing his decent. His hand brushed the wall only to find the plaster was damp. "You haven't seen any rats down here, have you? I hate rats."

Katherine was trying to pull at the ropes.

"I'm only asking because in that story in the magazine, there were rats in the room. This is the same room, isn't it?"

There were a couple of giggles as bodies and faces emerged from the darkness.

"Yes, it's the same room. Come on in, Hal."

"Well, if it isn't Davey from Dallas, or, should I say, the almost famous actor Samuel Cross. And there we have our little sweet little Zoe. How are you, dear? Typical Shakespearian tragedy, don't you think?"

"How's that?"

"Well, Davey, sorry, Samuel, we have you, the failed actor. Named by chance after a Shakespearean actor who died centuries ago? Tired of having the bit parts and watching others take the lead? Then we have Zoe, the typical woman in a Shakespearean play."

"What do you mean? I'm just me."

"Zoe, back then there were no women on the stage, so all the female characters were played by boys."

"I'm not a boy."

"No, Zoe, you're not. But you are a weak character with little to say who will be forgotten and abandoned before the final act."

"What?"

"It means as soon as he's used you, he will dispose of you."

"No, we is getting married."

"Shut it, Zoe."

"There it is. I bet you've heard that before. Nope, as soon as he gets the prize, he'll leave you at the closest nunnery."

"I'm not a nun."

"I said, shut it, Zoe."

"Yes, Zoe, I guess you should listen to him. I bet he's followed through before when you haven't, as he says, shut it. By the way, ask him what a nunnery means in a Shakespearean play. No? It means whorehouse, Zoe, whorehouse."

"But he said I don't have to do that no more."

Samuel turned and slapped Zoe across the face. As he did that, Hal struck out with a fist wrapped around the hilt of the sword. Samuel deflected the blow and moved quickly across the room.

"I brought one for you to use." He lifted a sword of his own. "How nice of you to bring one with your fingerprints all over it."

The two began to move throughout the room, touching their swords, tentatively engaging.

"Do you think you can beat me, Hal, my boy? I've played Romeo; I've played Henry; I even did a stretch as Hamlet. I know how to thrust and parry. What do you know?"

"I know you haven't found the chest yet. I know you can't kill anyone before you have it."

Samuel began to get a little more aggressive with the sword. "Then why don't you tell me, Hal my boy, before something has to happen to you or the pretty shrew you call Katherine."

"Not only do you not know where the chest is, I bet you have no idea what's in it."

"Treasures, Hal, treasures."

"Who told you that fairy tale?" Hal was beginning to have trouble with the way Samuel could swing his sword.

"An old librarian told me. She showed me the pin and told me the Broken Quill Society keep treasures here. Everything is in that chest. Just find it, and you're richer than you could imagine. She even told me about this hidden room underneath her old office. Then I learn that Katherine is going to announce all sorts of secrets here today, and I say to myself, Samuel, this is your payday."

"So, you do plan to kill her?"

"Nobody else can ever know, Hal. I helped plan it all out. I helped set up that magazine. By the way, you'd be surprised how many writers want to contribute as soon as a magazine is set up. I didn't even advertise, and they sent me stuff."

"And one of them wrote the story about me killing Katherine?"

"No, that was someone else. Pretty good work, don't you think? He's no Hemingway, but I think he did a good enough job to frame you."

Zoe was looking a little worried. "This is taking too long. Play the game like we're supposta do."

"That's right; thanks for reminding me. I still don't understand why he insists we do this."

"Who are you talking about?"

"Never mind that. Here's what we're going to do. I ask you some questions. If you answer them correctly, then maybe Katherine walks out of here alive. Deal?"

"Deal."

"Then come over to this table." Both took seats in leather-backed chairs and placed their swords within easy reach. "The first question for you, Hal, is why do you enjoy making locks of Katherine's hair?"

"You know that wasn't me, so what kind of a question is that?"

"What if could show you both a photo of you picking up hair from the trash bin outside a salon?"

"I would say that you're a worse poker player than I am. You're bluffing, so what's the next question?"

"Are you in love with Katherine?"

"No. I thought this was going to be an interesting game, so get on with it."

"I hear you've been sharing a room for the past couple nights, and all sorts of people have heard you fighting. You went out of your way to get her from the tower and now you're here. So, I'll ask you again, are you in love with Katherine?"

Hal gave Katherine a long look and chose his words carefully, as it appeared that only one answer would be correct in Samuel's mind. "Yes. Now that's settled, what's the next question?"

"Here's one that's harder. Did Thomas Bodley have a second iron chest? I caution you to think carefully and answer truthfully on this one."

"Yes. There is a second chest."

"Tell me where it is."

"That's not a question."

"You're beginning to really get on my nerves. What location will help you and Katherine walk out of here without the aid of medical attention?"

"The answer to that question is the location of the chest. Don't get mad at me; you're the one asking these questions."

"I'm only asking one more time and I'm not messing around here. Where is the second iron chest?"

"Is it really anywhere? Think about it; if nobody can see it, then does it exist anywhere but in our minds? If that's true, then when no one was thinking about it, it couldn't exist and our talking about it might not be enough to bring it back. In a way, it exists and doesn't exist at the same time. I say we forget about it, as in order to see it, we must first act as the creators of it."

"I really hate you people who went to university trying to make me feel stupid."

"I was just answering your question."

"Answer this!"

Within moments, both Hal and Samuel were standing and circling each other with the swords back in their hands.

"I've finished playing silly buggers with you, so just tell me where the chest is, and we'll get this over with."

"I can't help you any more than that, Sam. What else did that old librarian tell you?"

"The name is Samuel, not Sam. She told me to find the chest, and I would find the bones of William Shakespeare. Think about it, the bones of the bard. I could sell them for millions."

Hal stopped circling and lowered his sword. "That's just stupid. How could anyone steal his bones and put them in a chest? Everyone knows he's buried in Stratford-on-Avon."

"He was moved to Westminster Abbey, or don't you know everything?"

"Is that what you were talking about at breakfast the other day? You're partly right. They were thinking about moving him to Poet's Corner in the Abbey, but never went through with it. If those were the librarian's books upstairs in the office, then she loved gothic novels and all the strange stories that went with them."

"That sweet old librarian told me a story that's been kept secret for centuries. They dug up the bones to move them before they changed their minds and then the bones disappeared. It was Thomas Bodley himself who put the bones somewhere in that chest. And he buried the chest here in the library."

Samuel lowered his sword.

"What is it Hal? What're you thinking? You know where the chest is, don't you?"

"I'm trying to remember the poem on his grave in Stratford. How does it go again? 'Good friend, for Jesus' sake forebear to dig the dust enclosed here; blest be the man that spares these stones, and cursed be he that moves my bones'."

"Whatever, they were moved by that Bodley guy, and I know that for sure."

"I'm thinking that almost makes sense because if you ignore basic facts, it could have happened. I'm also thinking that would be a conspiracy story for the ages. Unfortunately, I'm also thinking that Bodley died first. That means, I'm thinking you're an idiot."

Samuel raised the sword again. "First, I'm going to run this through little Katherine, and then I'll watch as you get the blame. Remember, it's in the story you wrote. A copy was sent to you too early, but I sent one to the police here, and just in case, the police in your hometown. In fact, I put them out all over London. So tell me where the chest is, and tell me now!"

"I won't let you."

"Let me what?"

"I won't let you hurt her again."

"Who are you talking about? Zoe or Katherine?"

"I said, I won't let you hurt her again."

Katherine reacted immediately to that statement, and strained at the ropes holding her to the chair when it was repeated.

This time when they began to hit the swords, together there was more power and an urgency to win the battle. "That's a stage sword." Hal was still speaking in a calm, even tone. "It's as dull as a butter knife and never meant for any real use besides making noise on the stage."

"You still can't stop me then. You have the same thing."

"Nope, sorry, try again. I took this from a medieval display case on my way down here. It's the real deal."

Samuel put both hands on the sword handle and began to swing with increasing power while Hal did his best to ward off the blows.

"You're not smiling anymore, Hal. My sword's holding up just fine. What makes you think you can beat me?"

"I've had a few lessons."

"I've had years of practice. Enough that I know stage swords are built to last a long time. And long enough I know to sharpen it if I want to put it to real use."

"Yet, here I am."

"Zoe, take the gag out of Katherine's mouth for me, love. There you go. So, Kate, are you enjoying watching me kill your boyfriend? I'm afraid the original plan isn't going to work, after all."

"He's not my boyfriend, and don't you ever call me Kate."

"Oh, she's a testy one. After I'm done with you, maybe I'll give her that smack you're too much of a coward to give her." This time he swung his sword with as much power as he had. Hal parried, but the blow hit his sword with enough force to deaden the feeling in his hand.

Katherine watched as the sword fell from his grasp. "Run, Hal! Go get help before he kills you!"

Samuel raised the sword again, taking a left to right arc to get the blade moving at full power. Katherine screamed. Zoe closed her eyes.

Hal bent down and picked up his satchel and, as the sword started its downward motion, raised it. The blade cut into the leather and stuck.

For Samuel, it was the same as striking a brick and it was his turn to let go of the sword. Hal removed the blade and tossed the sword behind him.

"I think you dropped something, but I seem to have mine." He picked up the sword he'd brought.

Samuel watched the sword being raised. "I'm not just an actor. I make money wrestling on the side." He bent double and charged.

Hal intently watched him. He saw the charge begin, but instead of being worried, he was glad it was coming straight at him. Hal waited until the last second and moved quickly to the left. Samuel ran into the base of the stairwell and, instead of trying to confront

Hal without a sword, ran up the stairs. Zoe, trying not to cry, followed.

Hal turned his attention to Katherine and used the sword to cut the rope holding her to the chair. Just as he was successful, the sword broke at the handle.

"Something tells me that's a stage sword as well."

"So, I lied."

"And what if it broke during the fight?"

"Then someone could write the tragedy of Hal and Katherine."

"Get these ropes off my wrist."

He picked up the blade while Katherine raised her hands to allow him to see what he was doing in the poor light. As it was a dull stage sword, he had to use a great amount of force.

There was noise from the top of the stairs. "Hal! I hear someone coming!"

"I'm trying to hurry, but I don't want to cut you."

"Hurry!"

"Stop moving. If you don't, I'm going to stab you."

"You're not going to stab anyone. Just put the knife down." The voice came from behind Hal.

"I'm trying to cut the ropes."

"Put the knife down now!"

Blinded by the men's flashlights, Hal said, "First, it's not a knife, it's a sword blade. Second, I'm cutting through this rope, not stabbing her."

With the rope cut, Hal dropped the sword blade and turned to face the men crowding into the room. He found himself face down on the floor with his arms pinned behind his back.

"Let him go! That's Hal; he wasn't hurting me!"

"Calm down. It's all over."

"No, let him go!"

"He had a big knife to your chest. Calm down; we have him now."

Katherine grabbed the bulletproof vest of the closest constable. "I am calm, so listen carefully. That's my partner, Hal. He was helping me, so let him go."

The flashlights were shone over them one more time. "Let him up and get EMS in here. He's got a pretty good cut on his arm."

Katherine was taken upstairs by a group of constables.

Hal touched his arm, amazed by the amount of blood that soon covered his hand. He was removed from the basement and taken to a room separate from Katherine.

"The charge is attempted murder, so I want to make sure everything you're telling us makes sense."

"I'm telling the truth, constable."

"Professor Wales, please understand, we're laying charges against the appropriate individuals, so the facts have to make sense. This whole thing about a story in a crime magazine is a little strange. But we'll take a long look at that. Tell me again what they wanted here today."

"They wanted to know the location of Shakespeare's skeleton. Are you sure Katherine's alright? She was the one they wanted to kill."

"She's not hurt. From what I hear, she's making life hell for the other constables."

"Good. Now I know she's fine."

At last he was lead outside to the quadrangle and reunited with Katherine. The chairs were in disarray, and people were slowly starting to return from where they had been sent to for safety outside of the library complex.

Hal stopped one of the returning attendees. "Tell me about the fire."

"That may be the best news of all. It was started in a stairwell that was mostly stone. Lots of smoke, but no real damage. No books were burned."

Several constables approached in a tight group and, as they got closer, they revealed the three individuals who were walking in the middle. "Can you two say if you have seen these people before?"

Katherine spoke first while pointing. "These two men kidnapped me a couple days ago."

"Kidnapped?" Samuel was laughing. "You were more than willing to go with us. Don't forget, you're the one who wanted to see London from the tower. All I did was help a girl out. It's not my fault you drank that much."

"Help me! You wanted to throw me off it!"

"How? Did you look at the fence they have up top? Of course not; we never made it that far. If we had, then don't forget what you suggested we do at the top."

"And what about today, Sam? You wanted to kill me and Hal today."

"It's Hal and I. Some English professor you are."

"Don't you dare talk to me like that, Sam."

"Do not dare to call me Sam. The name is Samuel, Samuel Cross the famous actor the Bayonne Weekly once called the next great thespian of 1983." A constable tightened his grip on Samuel's arm, which successfully stopped any more exclamations of importance.

"What about you, Hal?" The constable looked at him. "Recognize anyone?"

"That one tried to steal my satchel, and then he was in the office I told you about in London. Sam's the one who tried to kill me with a sword just now. Oh, and someone tried to push us in front of a train at Victoria tube station."

"We didn't push anyone," Zoe said, looking at the other two. "Did we?" Both of the men shook their heads no.

Hal held up a finger to be noticed. "I never did learn that second's man's name, though."

"That would be Andy Player. Mr. Player is sort of well known to us, having made an appearance in many crimes. It seems nobody remembers him when it's finished, so he moves on to something else. We'll start by charging them all with unlawful detainment, attempted theft, and for setting fire to the library. The attempted murder charges will follow shortly." As the group moved on, Hal heard someone muttering, "Bloody Canadians. If they'd just stayed home, none of this would have happened."

Katherine accepted a bottle of water, deep in thought. She didn't immediately notice the plain-clothed sergeant who took Hal to one side. "I have something to talk to you about"

"I'll get Katherine."

"No. This only involves you, as far as I can tell."

"What is it?"

"London transit security officers say you two were involved with an incident at the Victoria tube station. They really didn't believe you, but kept looking at the security cameras and passed a photo on to us. Did they show you one?"

"Yes, but all you could see was a hat, not a face."

"They followed the wearer of the hat with other cameras and got a look at who was wearing it. We then checked it out with our databases and did a facial recognition search. I've got it on my phone; take a look."

"I'm sorry, but I don't recognize him. Who is he?"

"His name is Percy Northland."

"Northland, oh, of course. I haven't seen him for years."

"He's wanted internationally, as it turns out, but I wanted to know if he's had any connection to you. It took a bit of digging, but a friend across the sea found an old Canadian file that had your name attached, but didn't say why. How did you know him?"

"I was one of the people who testified against him in a trial. I was underage at the time, but he was the foster father in a group home I was in for a while in Canada. How'd he get here?"

"That's something we're trying to figure out. Apparently, he wasn't a model prisoner, so he did an entire ten-year stretch. After he was released, he disappeared and was believed to be working with the drug cartels in Mexico. Interpol became interested when he was linked to events in France. Somehow, he got through our security here in spite of that."

Hal thought of the pages of photos which had mysteriously appeared on his seat during the flight but decided to say nothing.

"So, I need to ask, have you had anything to do with him since he got out of jail?"

"If you're asking me if I have any connections to drug cartels, then the answer is a firm no. Does it look like he was involved with this group?"

"They did mention that there was somebody running the show, which makes sense. These guys couldn't plan something this complex."

"So you didn't get everyone then? I better tell Katherine."

"If you want to. I don't think Northland would have a reason to go after her, but if you put him in jail for that long, I'd recommend you watch your back."

"Yes, yes of course. Thank you."

The sergeant left, and Hal moved back to Katherine's side.

"What was that about, Hal?"

"Nothing. Nothing you need to worry about at all."

Chapter 19

"LADIES AND GENTLEMEN, could I have your attention." The speaker on stage was trying rather unsuccessfully to be heard by the returning conference attendees. "Ladies and gentleman, we do plan to hear the concluding speakers after a short break for us all. As scheduled, we'll hear from our keynote speaker, Dr. Katherine Minola, last. I think you'd agree that is the talk you don't want to miss. Please check the revised schedule now on the whiteboard at the entrance and be back for the first speaker in an hour."

Not only did people want to hear from Katherine, they wanted to hear now, and a large crowd began to surround her. Hal directed her back to the chair and stood in front of her. "You heard what was said just now, so please wait until later."

"I just want to ask her about her research."

"I bet you do. Is that a Yale tie?"

"Well yes, it is. You see, I think Dr. Minola and I have things in common with our research."

"I may be mistaken, but I always thought Yale alumni were bound by a code of behaviour that didn't involve harassing others."

"That's just rude."

"No. if I wanted to be rude I'd ask about the Yale Bulldogs. How's the team this year? Do you know bulldogs are incredibly inbred?"

"Well I never! Wait, what's that sound? Is she having trouble breathing?"

Hal bite his tongue as the concern was over Katherine's snorting.

"I'd like it if everyone took a step back and let her breathe for a bit." He watched the crowd dissipate. "Are you over your laughing fit yet?"

"I can't believe you said that about the Yale Bulldogs. Even I know better."

"Probably not the best thing to say. What do you think, Katherine? Go get some food and try to relax for a bit?"

"Yes, but there's something else first. That shirt of yours is torn and bloody, and we can't walk around with you looking like that."

"What do you have in mind?"

"Follow me."

The pair walked to the Divinity Hall where Katherine started looking at the shirts being used for that night's performance. She was particularly drawn to the military ones. "What size shirts do you wear?"

"Medium, sometimes. Small men's, sometimes."

"No, Hal, what size? You know, neck size?"

"I don't really know."

"Oh, we have to do some shopping. Stand here and let me hold these up so I can see if they'll fit."

"Katherine, this is embarrassing."

"Just stop it. There's nobody watching. Here, try this on."

"There's no change room."

"It's only a shirt. Alright then, I'll turn around if that makes you feel better." She admired some of the costume jewellery before turning back to Hal. "What's wrong?"

"I'm having trouble moving my arm. It's kind of stiff."

"Let me help put that on." She quickly helped and stood beside him for a moment, using her finger to trace the chevrons on the shirt. "If you hadn't found me…"

"But I did."

"I've never seen you like that before, Hal. I don't know what I would've done."

"You would have taken care of yourself, as always."

Katherine snapped from her reverie. "Of course, I would have."

"I would expect nothing less from you."

"Hey, you two! What do think you're doing!"

Hal looked at the same person who, earlier, had shown him the playbills. "We just needed a shirt. It's kind of a special circumstance."

"I'm not going to let you steal that."

"We're not stealing; we're just borrowing."

As they quickly headed for the exit to the quadrangle, Josie Parker ran to talk to them. "If there's anything you need..."

Katherine grinned. "It's a little late for that offer."

"Maybe not." Hal tilted his head sideways. "What do you know about the Broken Quill Society?"

Josie couldn't shake her head fast enough. "Don't say that. Not here in public. We'll talk after; in fact, we want to talk to you after everyone has left. But not now." She hurried away.

"Alright then, Hal, just when we thought it was over, they're back. What made you ask?"

"I'm not sure, and I can't think right now. I'm just too damn hungry."

"Anyplace particular you want to go?"

"The one place every Oxford student knows."

"The Pieminister it is."

Chapter 20

WITHIN MINUTES THEY were back on High Street where it was a short walk to the Covered Market, an area known for its small boutique shops, famers markets, and incredible butcher shops. It was also the home to a particular shop loved by Oxford students. There were only a couple of people sitting in the Pieminister at the long counter facing the window, and Hal could also see room at the handful of tables to the left of the entrance.

The young woman working the counter had smiled as they walked in.

Hal nodded, "What do you think, Katherine?"

"Oh, something vegetarian. I'll have the mushroom and spinach with mushy peas and a pot of tea."

"And for me, make it the beef and stilton, but load it up."

Hal watched as the pies were plated, with his pie sitting in mashed potatoes and topped with gravy, mushy peas, and a crunchy cheese and breading mixture.

As he needed to for expenses, he made sure to pocket the receipt before putting a five-pound note in the tip jar and earning another smile from the server.

"So, Katherine, are you going to tell everyone what we've been through as part of your presentation?"

"I have a feeling we're going to be asked, but how much to tell is the question."

"Is there something you don't want people to know?"

"More like, I don't want them to concentrate on how people tried to kill me, or us, I guess. I want them to listen to my finding about William Shakespeare."

"I'd agree with that."

"What was that idiot trying to say about the bones of Shakespeare? Does he really think the skeleton is hidden in the library?"

"He mentioned that an old librarian told him about the society and told him a story about bones buried here."

"Wonderful. Hal, maybe this Broken Quill group really wants to stop us."

He put the satchel on the table. Katherine grabbed it. "Oh no! Look at the cut in the leather. He sliced that sword right into the sun design. I hope this can be fixed. Maybe you should call Jarrod."

"I'm just glad he hit the sun and not my fingers."

"Well, using this for a shield wasn't the brightest idea. You know, it really does look valuable."

"I didn't have many options, if you remember." He took the satchel back from Katherine. "There's something more. I still have one thing to show you." Hal reached into the satchel's pocket and laid a strange medallion on the table. "Look at this. I found it between two slats in the bottom of a box."

"Alright then. About the same size as a good old Canadian loonie."

"Or a British two-pound coin."

"Right, just thicker. Inset on this side, we have what appear to be three keys. Wait, is this a stamp of some sort?"

"My guess would be a wax seal, Katherine. But I've never seen one like that. If it belonged to Thomas Bodley, then I would expect his initials or a family crest. Plus, on the other side there's a small hole. "

"Well, wax seals were sometimes watch fobs and I've seen a couple that went on the end of a dip pen."

"Katherine, what's the earliest version of the dip pen?"

"The quill. Oh, crap, are we back to quills again?"

"I think so."

"You know what this is, don't you?"

"I have an idea, but first you need to present your research. After all, I could be wrong."

"Let's head back then and see what happens, but first, another little side trip."

"The bathroom?"

"You've got it."

They had to ask for directions as it turned out that the regular washrooms were under renovations and the temporary ones were portables in a back lane normally only used for deliveries. Hal was the first to return to the back entrance to the Covered Market, where he quickly found himself in the way of transport vans, construction workers, and angry mothers attempting to get their children to the toilet on time.

He wandered down the back lane, checked his watch, and calculated the time back in Calgary. A recent graduate from Red Deer College had taken a job with the *Calgary Herald* newspaper as a fact checker, and Hal soon had him on the phone.

"That's right, Larry, same kind of murders with bodies left in the wall."

"Why do you think nobody has made this connection before?"

"Two countries, and very old crimes anyway."

"This could really help my career. Thank you so much Professor Wales. And you'll give me that book when you get back?"

"No problem. Oh, there is one more thing, though."

"Yes?"

"See if you can find occupations for his victims."

"Why is that?"

"Something tells me they may have all had the same line of work."

"What would that be?"

"Acting, Larry, I bet they were all actors."

He said goodbye, but knew it was time for the phone call he wanted to avoid. He checked the online City of London phone book and found the listing for Bathsheba Savage. He took a deep breath, hit the button, and listened to the double rings of the British phone system.

"Hello." The female voice sounded old and worn.

"Hi, I'm trying to reach Bathsheba Savage."

"Speaking. Who is this."

"Could you tell me if you were in a theatre group called The Queen's Men?"

"A long time ago. Who is this?" The voice had become higher and agitated.

Hal began to speak more slowly in order to keep control. "Did you make a trip to Canada?"

"Who is this?" This time the voice was a scream and Hal heard the phone dropped and the sounds of a conversation in the distance.

"Who is it that's calling, please." It was a new voice: female and strong.

"My name is Hal Wales."

"Get to the point or I'll ring off."

"Did Bathsheba, 27 years ago, did she…" Hal wasn't sure he could say it.

"Did she what?"

"Did she have a baby boy?"

"Exactly who are you?"

Hal bit the inside of his cheek. The sounds around him were mixed with voices in his head. "This is … this is the baby."

There was a silence, followed by the sound of the phone being put down and another hushed conversation.

"Are you in Canada?"

"No. I'm in Oxford, but I'm staying in London until tomorrow."

There was another moment of silence. "Where are you staying in London?"

"The Premier Inn. The one by Victoria rail station."

"If someone wants to talk to you, then we'll contact you there. If not, then I have to ask that you never call this number again. Do you understand me?"

"But I just need to ask…"

"I said, do you understand?" The voice had become stern.

"I understand, but…"

He heard the sound of the phone being hung up. He leaned against a brick wall, took out the bottle of pills from his satchel and, after looking at it for some time, threw it into a garbage bin. He wandered back up the lane where a portable card table had been set up and a game was underway.

Katherine joined him: "Alright then, I love a good game of three-card monty. Stay here. I'll be right back."

There were a couple of winners and one big loser before Katherine returned, and it was obvious what she wanted to do. "Do you know how to win at this, Hal? No? Well just watch and learn."

She approached the table. "Anyone mind if a lady tries her hand at this?"

"Not a problem for us. You know the way the game is played. Just find the queen and win the cash. What would you like to start with? One pound? Two maybe?"

"Katherine, we really need to get back."

"Nonsense Hal, this won't take any time at all."

"We're expected, remember?"

"Come on, buddy, let your sweetie have a go at finding the card."

Katherine checked her watch. "He's right; we really don't have any time to play."

"Just give it one shot, lady, and find out how easy it could be. Make it two pounds and have some fun."

"No, why don't we make it a hundred pounds and really have fun?" She laid the money on the table in a collection of ten- and five-pound notes. The dealer eyed it before adding another hundred pounds and placing a small rock on the notes to keep them from blowing in the light breeze.

"Here we go then, lady. Three cards: two of them black and the red queen of hearts. Watch the cards and not the hands as around they go to the left and to the right. Guess the right card and win double or nothing. Everyone watch carefully as there's only one chance to pick the winner, and if she can do, then so can you. So, lady what do you think?"

"This one here on the left."

"The left she says, everyone. Gather round and gather close as we play a clean game here, and I want you all to watch carefully as the card is flipped."

"I want to flip it, though."

"Of course you can flip the card, lady. That's how clean my game is. Just flip the queen and you win the pot."

Katherine had her left hand on top of the card and reached with her right hand to remove the rock from the pile of money. "I just flip this card and I get the cash." She lifted the rock slightly and the notes began to move in the breeze, forcing the dealer to grab them.

"Watch it, lady or we'll lose it all. Just flip the card."

"Alright then." Katherine flipped the card, exposing the queen of hearts as the dealer's hand went to a pants pocket; a look of concern crossed his face. She scooped the cash off the table and turned quickly. "Let's move, Hal. We don't want to be late." Hal followed and, although the dealer wanted to have a short chat with Katherine, he couldn't leave a crowd who wanted to see if they could also win.

"I have to say, that was pretty good. You managed to beat the dealer at a high stakes game."

Katherine snorted and, as they passed a garbage bin on the street, reached into her purse for a deck of cards which she tossed into the container. "I asked you if you knew how to win at three-card monty. There's only one way."

He put his arm around her and, laughing, they walked back to the Bodleian Library.

Chapter 21

"THERE'S STILL TIME to back out." They were standing in front of the entrance to the Bodleian Library. "Everyone would understand if you walked away."

"I've gone through too much to quit now."

They entered the quadrangle where the final presentations had already started, and joined fellow conference attendees sitting in the late afternoon sun. Others sitting in the group kept turning and whispering as they wondered what the last presentation would hold.

There was a short break for everyone to get a tea before Katherine was scheduled to begin. Hal fiddled with the lectern, trying to adjust it to the correct height. "I'm sure I saw a couple more of those quill pins in the crowd."

"So did I, Hal."

That was all there was time for before a moderator began the introduction. "Today has proven to be eventful, and it appears that there will be more to the story than we have heard so far. I wish to, once again, assure everyone that the criminals have been arrested, and there is no danger. That being said, let me introduce our final speaker. Dr. Katherine Minola comes to us from Canada where she is the Chair of the Department of English at Red Deer College. Red Deer, in the province of Alberta, is a smaller college with a superior reputation. Dr. Minola has published several articles and two books about theatre in the Elizabethan age. She now presents her new research titled *William Shakespeare: The Truth of the Lost Years, 1578-1582*. Please make Dr. Minola feel welcome."

Katherine took her place at the lectern and looked at the crowd. Hal had taken a seat in the front row just to her left side, willing to jump on the stage should anything more happen. He needn't worry; she was home. This was the environment Katherine loved.

"I would like to thank everyone for this warm welcome. It's certainly better than the welcome others gave me." There were grins at that comment "There've been many books written on where William Shakespeare disappeared to after he finished school in 1578. Many believed that based on his writing ability, he must have gone to university. However, no one has ever found the evidence. That is, until now."

The crowd leaned forward in their seats as Katherine elaborated on the details. "You see there were two facts which kept the details hidden for this long. William was never officially enrolled in any university. He was auditing classes and never stayed more than one term. He was there; then he was gone. He also used a pseudonym." She paused for a moment. "He used the name of John Falstaff." The murmurs were more than audible. "None of this is in any of the school records. It's like somebody wanted to keep it a secret."

Hal was looking directly at Josie Parker and saw her react before Katherine continued. "I looked at the records kept by the professors at the schools. They mentioned in their private class notes that they had one student auditing and they were instructed by university officials to allow that student to remain in the class but not test that student as that would create a record for official files. As a result, our dear William has a strong background in theology, political science, and history. He also studied languages including German, French, and Italian." At this point, people were trying to be discreet as they texted and emailed what they were hearing to colleagues around the world.

"But there is more to this, as you will imagine. Yesterday, Hal Wales, a top member of the Red Deer College teaching staff, and I did further research and began to put other details together. Hal, if you would."

A surprised Hal joined her on the stage. "I explained my findings to Hal and he had one more question. Who paid for this education? We worked together and found the answers. Hal, if you could explain our discoveries?"

Hal took his turn at the lectern. "William's father, John, was involved in the illegal importation of items from Europe, including Catholic books that the Protestant queen would not have allowed into England. We found the evidence that shows one of his clients was Sir Thomas Bodley whose name graces this venerable library."

Josie looked uncomfortable and turned and shook her head no to several in the crowd who had looked to her at the same time. Hal took notice, but continued. "Thomas Bodley had already been in Europe for two years when the Shakespeare family disappeared. It's our belief that William would have joined him there. Bodley would have paid any tuition fees to allow William to audit classes and any other required, let's also call them fees, to keep that information private. This would have been his way of paying John Shakespeare back for doing something illegal and being forced to run from the authorities. All of that is interesting, but I suspect it's not what you've waiting to hear. The real question you want answered is, why would any of this result in people wanting to kill Katherine? That's something we couldn't figure out for some time. Katherine, would you like to start with the answer?"

As he passed the lectern back to Katherine he met her eyes. They had both noticed the reaction from certain individuals in the crowd, including Karen May and Josie Thomas.

Katherine made sure she made eye contact with Josie before starting. "The truth is, the details we have just explained to you are not worth killing anybody to keep quiet. What the criminals who were behind the acts against Hal and I, as well as the fire in the library, wanted was something greater. They believed that the bones of William Shakespeare are buried somewhere in this library in a second black iron chest." Josie looked amused and started to relax. "In a way, they're correct." With that, Josie once again looked concerned. "Those bones are worth millions. If I'd given them the location of the chest, then they simply needed to kill me and frame Hal to get away with it. Apparently, Hal is jealous of my success so his killing me wouldn't have been a surprise. Is that true Hal?"

Hal's look of contemplation of the idea elicited laughs from the crowd and resulted in Katherine smacking him in the back of the head. At that, the laughter grew louder.

"You laugh now, but try working for her." As the laughter died down, Hal continued. "We're all aware of the famous black iron chest that Thomas Bodley used for valuables. However, Katherine has read the report of him taking possession of a second chest. This one has the same three-lock system, but has a plain exterior. It was meant to be hidden and preserve something for a long time." The crowd was on the edge of their seats, listening. "The question then becomes where would it have been hidden? This library was much smaller when Bodley ran it than it is now. We all know that. Over four centuries it has undergone renovations and yet nothing has been found. We all know that as well. Or do we? Who is the one person capable of having something at this library moved without records being kept?"

Eyes turned to Josie Thomas, but this time it was not a select few but the entire group who looked at her and forced her to respond. "I don't know anything. Well, I heard the stories, but that's all they were, right, stories?"

Hal looked at her for a moment. "What are the stories?"

"There're a few, but one is that there're some private documents that Bodley thought would be destroyed if they were ever seen hidden here somewhere. But I have to tell you, I have access to all the official records, and I've seen nothing about a real second chest. If I knew, then I'd tell everyone."

"I believe you." Hal looked at Katherine, who nodded in agreement. "I believe you don't know about it because there's no longer a reason to hide it from anyone. I also believe it exists." Hal closed his eyes. He could see the original plans for the library. He could see the well-known photographs of the renovations. He began to focus on more recent buildings, although those recent buildings were still hundreds of years old. "Come with me!"

Hal jumped off the stage and then turned to offer his arm to Katherine. The two were soon followed by everyone else, with Josie Parker running to be the first person behind the pair.

"Hal, are sure you know what you're doing."

"Trust me, Katherine; this is what I'm best at."

They lead the group into the Divinity School and then through another set of doors at the other end into a rectangular room with tiered seating on the sides and a large raised formal seat and lectern acting as the front of the room.

"Ladies and gentlemen, Convocation House." Hal smiled as he made the proclamation. "Please take your seats."

Everybody took seats on the benches and soon filled all the available spots. The chatter was constant, and Hal had difficulty signalling his desire to speak.

"Construction started, oh, when was that, Josie?"

"It was 1620 something. About 25 years after Thomas Bodley died. It was used for student convocations at the time and for some graduates, even today. And it was even home to the British parliament for a number of years."

"Has it ever been renovated?"

"A new ceiling was installed in the 1700s, but that was all."

"So, most of this room was not touched since it was built. Tell me Josie, as the head librarian, how far in advance do you plan renovations?"

"You watch the age of an area and condition it's in and make sure the funding is in place while hoping nothing happens you can't anticipate."

"Like what?"

"Like a roof leaking or a foundation crack. These are old buildings after all. That's why renovations get done, and that's how we know nothing was hidden around here."

"But if you wanted to hide something? What if you didn't want anyone to find it until long after you were dead? If that were the case, where would you, as the person in charge of everything, put it?"

"Now, just hold on a minute. I know what you want me to say here. You want me to say I'd stash it in the new building where it would remain secret the longest."

"And what about a renovated building?"

"There's still a problem with that. Who would know where it was originally? Who would know when it was going to be discovered and move it? And don't just say the head of library because we really don't know as much as you seem to think we know."

"Let's look at the basic facts. This has to do with John Shakespeare, not just his son. It has to do with Thomas Bodley, Catholic books, and a Protestant queen. Add to that, William who, as a playwright, could incite public riots with plays about the legal succession to the throne. We know a chest exists, and based on buildings and renovations times, I think the chest was moved to a safe location around a quarter-century after Thomas Bodley died. That's the time that makes sense. And where we are is the only location that works."

Josie was smiling as she began to inspect the seats and walls. Soon others were helping, hoping to be the one to find a hidden panel, but to no avail. "Everyone. Hands up. I don't want any damage done in here." Her directions were followed. "Hal, Katherine, what're we trying to find exactly?"

Hal looked at Katherine: "Tell them."

"It's a symbol. You want to find three keys. Hal will show you why later."

The group searched, but still found nothing. Hal, for his part, watched with amusement. At last he brought the search to an end. "If I remember correctly, the Oxford University chancellor sits here in the big chair at the end."

"That's correct." Josie added, "The lectern actually tilts forward as the chancellor, back when it was built, was rather rotund."

Hal tilted the lectern and bent down. "Here, under the seat where nobody would do anything but dust. Katherine, look at that."

Katherine joined him for a moment and then stood. "If you didn't look for an image of keys, you would think they were minor cracks in the wood. It's an engraving of three keys."

Josie Parker was the first of the group to look and she hurried out. By the time the others had taken their turn, she had returned with a gentleman holding a large wooden toolbox. "I would like you to meet Gregory. He's a master craftsman who specializes in renovations on woodwork centuries old. He often works late and on weekends to avoid being disturbed by the students. He came in today to look for damage caused by the fire. Nobody touches the woodwork around here without his approval."

Josie showed Gregory the small carving of three keys under the chancellor's seat. "We believe that there's something hidden under here, and we need you to open it up for us." All she received in reply was an emphatic shaking of the head to indicate no.

Hal stepped into the situation. "You're a lover of wood; I can tell that. I bet the tool chest you brought was handmade by a relative of yours generations ago." Gregory nodded the affirmative. "The woodwork in this room is exquisite. I bet you're one of the few people left who could make beauty like this." Gregory still said nothing but had a small smile on his face. "There is no way a master craftsman would hide something here knowing there was a possibility of someone needing to take a crowbar to it. What do you think?"

Gregory pulled a small chain from around his neck to show the medallion attached to it. Katherine was the first to realize what it was. "That would be Joseph, patron saint of carpenters."

He nodded and began to inspect the chancellor's chair in detail. He ran his hands on the wood under the chair and inspected the stairs leading to it. Finally, he sat in the chair and played with the movable lectern before standing. Placing both hands on the lectern, he began to use his weight and muscle to push straight down.

Josie Parker was watching intently, knowing that unwarranted damage could cost her the position as Bodleian librarian.

Gregory leaned to put more of his weight on the lectern. It was then that they heard it, the scraping of metal on metal. Hal grinned as the lectern slowly sank under Gregory's weight. Gears that had not moved in hundreds of years were pushed into action with an unclimatic popping sound. The floor boards on one of the broad steps released, and he stepped from behind the lectern to pick them up.

Hal looked down at the top of a black iron chest covered in centuries of grime. With Gregory's help, they found the handles on each end and pulled it out of its resting place to sit it in the centre of the floor. The chest was three feet long, two feet wide, and two feet deep. As the group moved to touch it, Hal noticed that Gregory replaced the boards and pulled the lectern up. The sounds of the gears resetting the locking mechanism weren't heard over the excited chatter of those watching.

"Everyone, everyone please stop talking." Josie Parker slowly got the attention of the group. "Please take your seats." The group obliged, but each examined the bench they were to sit on in hopes of finding another hidden compartment.

As Josie sat, Hal and Katherine stood on either side of the chest. Hal began, "We have no doubt that this is Thomas Bodley's second black iron chest, which brings us to two questions."

Katherine continued. "What's in it? And then there's the perplexing question of how do we open it?"

Hal pointed to the top front of the box. "Here we have three locks. The plan must have been that three people must present their key in order for the chest to be opened. My guess is we have one of them. Josie?"

Josie held up a long black key, similar in design to a church key. "There were certain things passed to me when I accepted the role of head librarian. My predecessor couldn't tell me what this was for as nobody had been able to tell him. It's just something that has been passed on to every new librarian. When I went to fetch Gregory, I picked it up from my office." She motioned to give it to Hal, but Hal held up a hand to stop her.

"That's only one key and we need three. I'm afraid my guess would be that the other two keys are lost to time." He waited for the noise of the crowd to dissipate. "However, there is a third question to be asked. How would Thomas Bodley put items in this chest without anyone noticing?"

"Well, certainly," Karen May said, rising from her seat, "he would not have given out the keys until the chest was full."

"That would make sense, but I think what this chest contains was sent to him over a number of years. He needed to protect what he had from harm, but needed to open it from time to time."

Katherine held up the small disk. "On this, what appears to be a wax seal, is the imprint of three keys."

"And here," Hal pointed to the top front of the chest, "is the same symbol but in reverse. If we take the seal, we find it matches and fits together."

Katherine demonstrated before handing the seal to Hal. Hal showed the other side. "On this side, we have a hole. I suspect the seal was once attached to something so it could be pressed into the chest as a lock bypass. Gregory, what do you think?"

Gregory took the seal and examined the hole before placing his hands on the top of the chest. He ran his hands over the top and then took a measuring tape out of his work chest and began to make notes. He went back to his work chest and took out a selection of dowels before finding one about the length and diameter of a modern pencil. With a small bladed knife, he cut and trimmed one end to produce an even smaller stub. With a dab of glue on the stub, the wax seal was attached, and he indicated with two fingers the length of time before he would give it to Hal.

The group was silent in anticipation of what would come next. When time expired, Gregory handed the seal on its new handle to Hal.

"I guess it's put up or shut up time. Let's find out, shall we." Hal pressed the seal into the impression on the chest. He pressed a little harder, and then contemplated asking someone else to try as nothing happened.

Gregory tapped the top of the chest and then, putting the palm of his hand in the centre of it, signalled Hal to try again. "Of course, a pressure sensitive lock when the bypass is being used." This time the wax seal with the symbol of the three keys began to move into the chest. Hal felt it reach the end after a couple of inches and looked back to Gregory as still nothing else was happening. Gregory continued to smile and made a twisting motion with his free hand. Hal turned the dowel to the right and heard the sound of three locks releasing their hold inside the lid.

"So, Gregory, master carpenter and locksmith then?"

Gregory, his job done, picked up his work chest and left.

"When Katherine and I were battling the criminals who wanted this chest, they made the comment about this containing the bones of William Shakespeare and then referred to the chest as his tomb. They were partially correct, as Katherine mentioned. We know that the royal family were not impressed by some of his work, especially when he questioned who the rightful ruler would be after Elizabeth's death. He needed to protect his work and who better than his old friend Thomas Bodley to help? This chest is not the tomb of Shakespeare, but the chest of Shakespeare's tome." Hal motioned to Katherine and together they lifted the lid. "Ladies and gentlemen," Hal continued, "William Shakespeare, his works."

Josie Parker prevented the crowd from pulling everything out of the chest. She immediately moved in front of it with her arms outstretched. "Just stop! We do this correctly, or I will have this moved to another location and nobody will see anything. You there, find a cloth and wipe down that bench. You there with the phone, stop calling people and make sure to video everything. I want this up on YouTube so everyone in the world knows about it. Nothing here is going to be a secret for a moment longer." She took a pair of cotton gloves from a pocket and put them on before looking into the chest. "The first manuscript to be taken out, and no doubt the last to be put in, is, *The Tempest*."

Over the next few minutes, the contents of the iron chest were laid on the benches. Katherine had taken the fourth manuscript out and announced its title when all in the room realized it was a play they had never heard of. There were several more like that to follow. There were also letters indicating that Bodley had kept the correspondence he had with William.

Hal and Katherine sat on one of the higher benches as the manuscripts and letters were placed back in the iron chest so it all could be moved to a better location, much to the protests of the group. Katherine leaned against him and, once again, traced the chevrons on the shirt he was wearing.

"People, people, please! Let me speak." Their attention turned to Josie. "First we must catalogue every item. That will be rushed. We must authenticate every item. That will be done in record time as I bet every expert in the world is going to be booking flights to Oxford tomorrow." The crowd chuckled at that. "And then the most exciting part. We are a reading library. It's our job to make any book in our collection available to any person willing to come here and ask to read it." She paused for a moment and looked up to Hal and Katherine. "So, book your spots at the reading carousels now. There's going to be long wait to see these once word gets out." With that, she led the entire procession out of Convocation Hall and towards the section of the library responsible for cataloguing all new items.

Chapter 22

HAL AND KATHERINE were left sitting on the highest bench. "Hal, it's over, except for writing the book that will make our careers. And I mean both of our careers."

"No, it's far from over."

"How so?"

"You've forgotten about the Broken Quill Society. We still need to find out about them or it or whatever the Broken Quill Society is."

"Right. I saw the reaction from Josie when you asked about it. Any thoughts on the matter?"

"I have a few, but what I'm thinking right now about involves a hot bath and a bed."

"Oh, that does sound lovely." They both jumped as Karen May sat beside Hal. "Do you like a bubble bath where we watch all the bubbles disappear one by one?"

"Ms. May, I hardly think you're being appropriate." Katherine's back had straightened and her lips pursed.

"Appropriate for whom, Katherine? Someone my age? Hal, I could teach you a thing or two."

"Hal, are you going to stand up for yourself?"

"Why are you asking him to stand up to me? This young professor can do anything he wants. Unless there's some reason you think he shouldn't? Hmmm Katherine?"

"Of course, he can do whomever, I mean whatever, he wants. I just think he has better options."

"Like you?" Karen turned her attention back to Hal. "Methinks the lady doth protest too much. How good are you at giving back rubs? I give a really nice one. I learned how when I was working in Japan for a few years."

"Hal, I think it would be best if we left."

"Actually, Hal, I think it's best if you and Miss Prissy Pants there kept your bums on the seats."

"Hal, let's go." Katherine stood up.

"Sit your bum back on that bench, missy. You asked a few too many questions about a certain group and now you get the answers. And by the way," Karen again spoke to Hal, "the bubble bath and back rub offer stands."

For his part, Hal was too busy watching something else to pay much attention to Karen. Several people who had been part of the group at the conference were slowly returning. Each would enter, look to where Hal and Katherine were sitting, and then find a place on one of the benches. Around fifteen had sat down when Josie Parker entered and closed the large doors behind her. She then locked the doors and proceeded to sit in the chancellor's chair. All eyes were on her as she stood to address the small gathering.

"Good evening, and welcome to this historic meeting of the Broken Quill Society. Although we were scheduled to meet anyway, the events of the day have turned this gathering into something else. Hal, Katherine, I must ask that you stand before me."

Katherine took Hal's arm and the two made their way to the spot which had been indicated.

"First, a little background so you understand who we are. Sir Thomas Bodley lived in fear of another Reformation. The first in England saw the destruction of almost all manuscripts held in the original library. He formed this society to prevent the destruction of the collections if anything like a Reformation were to happen again. He called together only those who loved the written word as much as he did. He called together those who dedicated their lives to the preservation of words. He called together those who would risk everything to keep knowledge accessible to all. As years passed, others were recruited to join, but only after they had proven themselves to be worthy of membership in this society. We are the head librarians, the curators of special collections, and the founders of charities to preserve books. We have members in police departments and government offices. And yes, in case you were wondering, we do wear the pin which indicates membership in the society."

Hal took the pin out of his satchel.

"That's a cheap version of the real thing. We keep our pins hidden, often under a lapel, but if shown to another member, it allows instant access to libraries and collections around the world. Those who are here, you must understand, are but a few of the members from around the world. This was to be a meeting discussing budgeting and a new software system for tracking recent allocations in libraries, so not that many needed to attend. Many are going to regret missing this meeting, I can tell you that."

Hal tried not to notice that Karen May had changed seats and was waving her fingers at him.

"The head of the Bodleian Library is always given the honour of being the head of the society. Although we are worldwide, that is one aspect of the society that has never been changed. What has changed is that there is now a board of directors. Each director is in charge of a country and keeps track of the changing laws. Usually, that has to do with taxes for libraries and how charity funds must be maintained. Mind you, there are certainly enough countries where books are at risk. When that happens, we work with the director to transport books and documents to a safer country until the danger passes. You should have seen how many items were taken out of Canada during the last world war. You might not have had any battles on Canadian soil, but the politics of the country almost lead to government-ordered book burnings."

Murmurs were heard from the older society members who knew the history that many Canadians didn't.

Josie waited for silence before continuing. "What we, as a society, actually do for the public is not something debatable in any way. We were also given our mandate from Thomas Bodley. We are to protect and preserve and make available any book that a person wishes to read. The only modification has been in the definition of what a book or document is."

She looked at Hal and Katherine and grinned. "Let's face it, there's no way Bodley could have anticipated electronic publication, but we work on preserving those as well. I think the problem with the iron chest was, where do you draw the distinction between protecting and making works available? I suspect the librarian who moved it had no idea what was inside. I imagine he was just following his understanding of the mandate because, if Bodley kept it hidden, then that's what had to continue. Darn it, Karen, would you stop blowing kisses at him! Do you remember that happened the last time?"

There were chuckles throughout the room, and Hal realized he was not the first young professor who had attracted Karen's advances.

"Normally, there's a process that can take up to five years after an individual is proposed for membership. It involves testing and background checks that result in only ten percent of proposed members actually being told about the society and being invited to join. I contacted the board of directors when I realized you knew something about the society. It was left to me to make the final decision and, given what you uncovered today, I only have one option. I doubt it's one that anybody will oppose. Hal, Katherine, we offer to you membership in the Broken Quill Society. Would you accept?"

"Yes," was the joint reply.

"Do you then promise to follow the mandate as given to us by the society founder to protect and preserve and to make available everything to those who request to see it, be it book, journal, letter, or any other form?"

"Yes."

"Do you also promise not to mark, deface, or injure in any way any book, document, or any object under our protection."

"Yes."

"Then I present to the gathering the newest members of the Broken Quill Society."

The applause was stopped by Karen raising her hand. "Those who are asked to join always have specific talents that we can use. You two are academics with the ability to research and discover. We would like to ask you to become our investigators should, and if, a need be found. Do you accept?"

Katherine squeezed Hal's arm while he placed his own hand on hers. "Yes," was once again the simple response.

"Katherine, Hal, welcome to the Broken Quill Society. Oh, we'll also supply you with a pin. It has been recommended, and I agree, that yours should be a different metal so other members will know your role. I assure you, you will have immediate access to any location where a member works."

She watched as others in the room prepared to leave. "Then we are done for tonight. The light is failing anyway, and we soon won't able to see each other. To those who are here for the budget meeting, we'll have that tomorrow at 11am at the Pieminister. Those of you who are here to talk about the new software, please be in room 15 at noon and bring your laptops. That said, Katherine and Hal arrived in Oxford by bus. Could someone from London please drive them back to their hotel and no, Karen, I was not thinking of you so please put your hand down."

The night's production of *Henry IV* was underway, and the Divinity School had several people in it. The society members went through another exit that first went into a small room featuring a large square table with bleacher seating on three sides. Hal pointed to it. "You remember what this is for?"

Katherine was laughing. "The Oxford University courtroom. I wonder if we'd be sitting here if things ended differently." The courtroom had been used until the 1970s for student crimes, which included missing curfew and talking back to professors.

They were finally taken out a back door leading to a staff parking lot.

"There he is. I want that man stopped right now." The group looked over at the same person who had been looking after the costumes in the Divinity School. "First he takes a playbill and doesn't pay for it, and then he comes back and takes a shirt. Look, he's still wearing it. Do you have any idea how difficult it was to have another one that small made on time?"

Josie attempted to intervene. "There've been some events today. You may have heard about them?"

"I don't care. That playbill was worth two pounds and that shirt's worth a good twenty."

The group dug for coins in their pockets to pay him. "See, it isn't that difficult. The next time you think of borrowing something, you remember this. There's no reason anybody should just walk in and take something like you did. Oh, I'm just going to borrow it, you say. You want to leave, do you? Well, just remember not to borrow things anymore. And for that matter, don't lend anything either, as that's the fastest way to lose everything. And you really need to get better clothes as they can tell people who you are. And make sure to listen to people, but don't believe everything they say."

He tried to continue, but Josie took his arm and walked him back to the university. There were still a few more handshakes and backslaps before Hal and Katherine were escorted to a car for the drive back to London.

"I'm so excited." The lights of Oxford were a few minutes behind them. "I don't think I'll sleep at all tonight."

"Not me, Katherine; I bet I'll be out before my head hits the pillow."

"You were quite impressive. In you charged with a sword. I just loved that. That was strange when Gregory didn't say a word, don't you think?"

"He's one of those guys who let his work speak for him. I bet he came from generations of master woodworkers."

"What did that police officer want to talk to you about?"

"Boy, you're all over the place. He just needed to confirm my home address and phone number."

"I've been meaning to ask you about your parents. Do you really not know who they are? I couldn't figure out if Jarrod was lying half the time."

"No, I don't know. For as long as I can remember, I was in group homes and foster homes."

"You must want to find out, though?"

"Let's not talk about that. What about you? Where did you spend your childhood?"

"I grew up in and around Toronto. My mother died from cancer when I was young and my father was in the Canadian military. He couldn't take me with him when he was sent on peacekeeping missions and other things, so he would leave me with his sister and her husband."

"That must have been a little rough."

"Not really. My aunt and uncle are really good people, and dad came home every chance he could so we could spend time together."

"Where is he now?"

"He's retired and living in Orillia. I go out to see him when I can."

There was a slight vibration in Hal's pocket. Hal pulled out his phone and checked the text message, although it was a moment before he realized what he was seeing.

Let Henry's son on holy ground be set

Before the sparrows find their so sweet voice

His blood not spilt soon is turned into jet

This, not his, but from another's made choice.

Hal leaned back and closed his eyes. The troubles were not over.

"Was that someone from work?"

"No, it was a personal message. Do try and relax, or you won't go to sleep at all."

It was another hour before they were in front of their hotel rooms.

"I guess we don't need to share rooms anymore. Sleep well, Katherine. I'll see you for breakfast as planned, so we can get to the airport on time."

"Good night, Hal."

Hal entered his room, but ten minutes later Katherine knocked. She had changed into a very short black dress that accentuated her curves.

"Katherine? What is it? Is something wrong?"

Katherine said nothing for a moment while her mouth moved as if trying to find the words. She walked to him and touched the chevrons on the sleeve. "Call me Kate."

"Ah, yes then, Kate."

"Hal, I've been thinking…I mean we have been through so much and…well…I've just been thinking that, you know…maybe?"

"Katherine, you know I was only saying what he wanted to hear when I said I loved you."

"Are you sure? It sounded real to me? Perhaps we could, you know…"

"I think you may be tired and not thinking straight right now."

Katherine walked around the room, picking up items from the desk in her nervousness.

"What's this? Hal, what on earth is this?"

"That? It's a business card."

"Whose number is on the back? Who is this Veronica person and why do you have her home phone number?"

"She works at Harrods. I was asking questions about the pin, and she helped me out."

"What else did she help herself to? I can't believe that I'm here like this and you've been seeing someone else."

"I'm not seeing her, and I don't see why you're suddenly upset."

"You know why I'm angry. I'm taking my things and leaving." Katherine attempted to pick up all her belongings but, finding it impossible to balance them, gave up. "I'll get the rest later. Just open the door so I can leave."

Hal was uncertain what he could do to comfort her and simply held the door open.

"Well, Hal, is there anything you want to say before I leave?"

"Have a good night?"

"How dare you."

Chapter 23

"WHAT THE HECK is this?" Hal turned on the light to find a single sheet of paper with lines of poetry. "Did I fall asleep after all? Who managed to get into the room and put this on my pillow?"

He went to the washroom and, after filling the sink with icy water, plunged his face in it. A couple of minutes later, he sat at the desk and pulled out the other pieces of paper and the phone text message. "Let's add this last one and see what we have."

How does the soldier stay not known to time?

He guards the door from within for the God

Who lets you repent your oldest known crime

In the abbey where the thousands have trod.

Forgiveness comes for those who try to learn

The battles raged from London town today

To Oxford's shrine that is never to burn

The hero returns with the feet of clay.

Let Henry's son on holy ground be set

Before the sparrows find their so sweet voice

His blood not spilt soon is turned into jet

This, not his, but from another's made choice.

If cowards run, then let speed be too true

Dear Hal, if brave, this be for only you.

"This looks like one of the worst student poems I have ever seen. Let's figure out if there's anything to it. After all, that's why Katherine pays you the big bucks right? It's got a rhyme scheme, ten syllables per line so it's pentameter, and a stress pattern of...there is no stress pattern to the syllables. It is just like a bad student poem. Wait, it was given to me in three chunks of four lines and this last piece is a rhyming couplet. Fine, someone gave me a sonnet and a Shakespearean one at that."

He reached into his satchel for a pen and paper. "Let's see what this writer was trying to tell me. A soldier not known to time is the Unknown Soldier, and the abbey must be Westminster Abbey where the tomb of the Unknown Soldier is just inside the main doors. That was easy. These next four lines are all about the last couple days where there was a battle in London that went to Oxford's shrine, which has to be the Bodleian Library. So far, this writer is not saying that much. The third quatrain tells me that, oh, that's Henry's son, is it? In Shakespeare's *Henry IV*, Henry's son is Hal. This is about me. I have to be on holy ground before the sparrows sing and sparrows start singing at dawn."

Hal moved a curtain and peeked at the darkness. "I don't want to even think about that blood turning jet black part. But the ending is clear: if I'm not a coward, then I better show up. It says meet someone at dawn at Westminster Abbey and come alone. Would it have been so difficult to just say that?"

It only took half-an-hour before Hal was near the entrance of Westminster Abbey. He had to look down, as some of the paving stones were uneven and could trip an unwary traveller.

"How nice of you to make it."

A flock of sparrows made their way from one of the few trees in the area to a rooftop before beginning their morning hunt for food. Hal could make out the figure in the white Tilley hat who was standing beside the Handel memorial statue.

"I take it you're Percy?"

"And you would be little Hal, the boy who couldn't keep his mouth shut. How nice to meet you again after all these years. I wasn't sure if you could put together the clues in the sonnet. So, what did you think of it."

"It was, how did Samuel always put it, brilliant. I am going to guess you also wrote the story about me killing Katherine."

"Yes, that was me. How is your girlfriend, by the way?"

"She's not my…. Oh, never mind. What do you want?"

"I just want to talk. I thought this whole plot was a great way to get rid of you, but I sent the sonnet just in case something went wrong. It's so hard to get good associates these days. You see, Hal, I spent ten years in jail because of what you did that day. Ten long years thinking about what you'd cost me. I used my time productively, though. I got a couple degrees in science and engineering through an online university, and, for a laugh, I picked up an English degree as well. They've proven valuable in my current occupation."

"Drugs, I'm guessing."

"Little Hal, you make it sound so mundane. 'High end chemical pharmaceuticals that have a tendency to be rather addictive' would be a better description."

"Wait a moment. Are you behind this berry drug?"

"The berry drug? Is that what it's being called on the street? I hate that. I wanted it called Saskatoon just like those sweet berries we get back home. Nice sweet little things that make the perfect pies and jams."

"And now the perfect drug that kills people."

"Only if they misuse it, Hal. And that's not my problem."

"So how'd you go from that to all of this?"

"In my travels, I ran into this little group who wanted help looking for a chest. I thought the story about Shakespeare's bones was utter nonsense, but the others believed it so much I knew it was a good way to get rid of you altogether. I must say, you do have some deductive powers after all. It would have been a disaster if she'd died at the tube station that day."

"That was you, then."

"No, it actually was the drunks in the crowd who pushed you on the platform. I was just on my way to Soho."

"What about the bathroom at Harrods? You could've killed me there with that homemade poison gas."

"Poison gas? Are you making up another one of your stories? I've heard you've had some trouble with fantasies again. You sure did the night you called the cops on me. But, you know, I might have a product or two that could help with that. Or make the stories seem all the more real, if you prefer."

"Excuse me, gentlemen." The pair looked at a short, elderly nun who appeared to be on the verge of being blown away by the breeze. "We have a small church over here, and we have hot tea and some Welsh cakes if you'd care to join us."

Percy became the epitome of a true gentleman. "Oh sister, I thank you for your kind offer, but I'm afraid this old sinner doesn't belong in a house of worship."

"We don't want to talk religion or bring you back to the fold. Our mission is just to make sure everyone has a smile and a full stomach when they leave."

"That is so kind of you. Hal, I say we join the nice sister and have a spot of tea."

Hal was a little puzzled. "You're not worried about people seeing you? There're security cameras everywhere and I can just shout for help."

Percy took him by the arm and lowered his voice so the nun couldn't hear. "Now, Hal, I never travel alone, and you wouldn't want this sweet little nun to have any problems, would you?"

They followed her to a church that was only a couple of blocks away. The basement had a small kitchen and several tables filled with a handful of London's street people. Another elderly nun gave them Styrofoam cups of tea and a few cookies that had just come out of the oven.

"You know, some of these homeless guys could be here because of the stuff you make."

"That's not my problem, so if you want me to feel sorry for them, it's not going to happen. Tell me, Hal, did you ever feel bad about what you did to my wife? You remember, your foster mother? The other one you put in jail."

"Everything happened so fast after that night it's like a bad dream. I never did hear anything about either one of you after I had to go to court. Where is she?"

"Dead. They claim she slipped going down the stairs for breakfast, but there's no way that's the truth. If I ever find out who did it then I'll get some revenge there as well."

"I'm sorry to hear that. She was always nice to me."

"She's dead because of you, so never forget it."

They both ate another cookie while Hal watched closely to make sure he wasn't in any immediate danger. It was only when Percy appeared calm that he ventured to ask more questions. "This whole making a crime magazine to frame me just seems like a great deal of work to go to even if you want revenge."

"I could have taken care of you any time I wanted, but where's the fun in that? Ten years of going through the options gave me all sorts of ideas, like I said. Then I find out you're some sort of an English professor and it became clear. Make you pay by having your life destroyed. Kill her and put you in jail thinking about it for days after days and years after years."

Hal reacted to that. "So you still want to kill Katherine?"

"No. This plot failed, but you love stories, so I think I'll come up with a better one. Any other silly questions?"

"I know Andy drew the pictures, but I'm guessing you left me the photos in the plane and the locks of hair as well."

"Hal, you need to understand that in my profession I meet a large number of people and many of those people will do anything I ask of them. All I have to do is wave a little sample of my pharmaceuticals in front of them and just that fast, I get what I ask done."

"What now? We just walk away from each other?"

"Yes. I need to travel for a spell taking care of business, but you'll always be in my thoughts. See you back in Canada."

Hal watched as Percy walked over to the nun and put a large wad of bills in her hand before quickly leaving. He waited a few more minutes before giving everything in his wallet to the same nun and heading back to the hotel. He walked slowly this time and didn't bother to look over his shoulder.

Chapter 24

"HAL, THERE YOU ARE. I knocked on your door three times. We were supposed to go out for breakfast together, remember? Did you go without me?"

"I wasn't at breakfast, and I don't think a hotel hallway is the best place to talk at this time of day."

"Really? Don't forget we've a plane to catch, and I need to get packed. So, bring the rest of my things over and let's get moving."

"Watch what I'm doing. I'm opening the door. There, now you can go in and get your own things."

Katherine hurried in for the items she hadn't been able to carry the last time. "Hal, look, if this is about last night, then maybe I should say something."

"Nothing happened last night."

"You're darn right nothing happened last night, and don't you forget it. I don't want to hear any stories when we get back to work because nothing happened."

"You're right, nothing happened, and yet you keep talking about it. Katherine, I'm going to have a shower and then pack."

"We'll be late."

"No, you won't. You get to the Gatwick Express at Victoria on time. If I'm late, there'll be another train minutes later, and I'll see you at the airport. Now if you'll excuse me, I'm going to get undressed."

It was some time after she left that he read the final version of an email that needed sending: "Dear Doctor, I've thrown the pills away. The episodes won't be a problem any longer. I have met my enemy, my Moriarty, if you will. We will meet again, I'm sure, but as for now, I stand victorious."

He tried to ignore the fact that he was sitting in a corner, trembling ever so slightly.

*****

IT WAS A KNOCK on the door that brought him to his feet and the short whisper in his ear that caused him to follow.

He was soon sitting in a small café that was not yet open to the public with two middle-aged women looking at him with suspicion. "We need to make sure you are who you claim before anything else happens. Tell me again about where you grew up."

They had introduced themselves, but Hal was still unsure who was Gilda and who was Rose. "Gilda..." There was a shaking of a head. "I mean Rose. Look, ladies, I've already explained to you how I grew up and what lead me to look here. I mean, I can't think of anything more."

The two women looked at each other before one motioned to a car outside the café. Hal stood as the women entered. She was slightly shorter than he was, with fading red hair braided and held together at the end by a dark purple ribbon. She reached out for a moment before looking as if to faint.

Gilda and Rose reacted with haste and helped her to sit while she gathered her breath.

"My name..." She swallowed again and then looked directly at Hal. "My name is Bathsheba Savage."

"Then, are you..."

"Yes."

Hal reached out, wanting to embrace her, but saw her react in fear. Either Gilda or Rose put a hand on his shoulder to stop him. "She's not well, you see."

"I have so many questions. I don't know where to start."

"Take it slow, Bethy. Remember what we agreed. You can leave at any time."

"I wasn't married. And I just wanted to act. I wanted so badly to act. I had to keep it all to myself, the pregnancy and all to myself."

Ha said nothing. He barely breathed.

"They knew I was pregnant. The players, that is. They knew, but they couldn't help me much. Anyway, it was after a performance that I started…I mean you started…it was all so fast."

"Easy, Bethy. Take it slow."

"I was going to put you up, you know, have you adopted then, but I couldn't…I mean I saw you and I couldn't. So, I keep you and we went to Canada and then at the hotel…I mean at the hotel it started up again…"

"Here, love, have a cuppa and relax a little."

"But I have to ask him! I have to know!" She looked directly at Hal. "Do you ever…have you ever…had a problem with…" She looked bewildered and lost.

"Have I ever been overwhelmed by a darkness?"

Gilda and Rose both were startled by that that. Bathsheba looked up and meet Hal's eyes. "Yes. Baby boy, yes."

"I have. They told this could be hereditary. So, I've always wondered about you."

"And I, you. It had happened before, but that night at the hotel became worse. It was a bad performance. Lines forgotten and cues missed and the house was small so there was little money from the gate and the hotel wanted payment and then it all came again."

Gilda and Rose tried to settle her down but it didn't work.

"No, let me finish. I have to finish. This darkness came, and all I could see was danger. Danger for me, yes, but danger for you as well. The others, they were sneaking out the back door and I knew…I just knew I couldn't protect you, baby boy. So I wrapped you up and I left you. God help me, but I had to leave you behind. Forgive me. God, baby boy, please forgive me."

This time Hal did embrace her, and they stayed in the embrace for some time.

"I have so many other questions."

Gilda or Rose shook her head one again. "Not now. She can't take any more. You have to realize that afterwards, I mean when she got home, there were issues."

"She was committed. Sometimes the medications help, but it doesn't last, and then before you know it…well, we try to help. We acted back in the day and knew her then. So, we help out now."

"But there's one question…"

"Not now."

"I have to catch a plane home very soon. One question. Please!" He followed them outside to the car.

"She can't answer right now, but maybe we can help."

"I just need to know. What's my name?"

Gilda and Rose looked at each other. They both began to speak as if finishing each other's thoughts would clarify the matter.

"We thought you knew…"

"…from the forms you said you had…"

"…and the nurse…"

"…right, don't forget the nurse…"

"…so we thought you would know…"

"…we were wrong…"

"…oh, yes wrong…"

"…but you see…"

"…you understand…"

"…you don't have one…"

"…well, sort of…"

"…sort of…"

"…the only thing she called you…"

"…then…"

"…and now…"

"…yes, even now…"

"…was baby boy…"

"…yes, baby boy…"

"Stop talking! Just stop a moment here." He heard it then: the voice coming from the car.

"You're my baby boy. My little baby boy."

"Later, when she's able."

"We'll call."

"I understand." The car left, but he stood watching the street for some time.

$$*****$$

AS A RESULT, Hal didn't make the next train, or the one after. By the time he arrived, Katherine was not amused. "It's about time you got here. What'd you do, use up all of the hot water in the hotel?"

"Let's just say I wasn't in much of a rush."

"Well, if you look at the ticket they gave you, you'll see I upgraded your ticket to first class so we can sit together."

"I can hardly wait."

"What's with you today? After everything we discovered, we're going to be academic darlings forever. There'll be books and articles and interviews and television appearances. I even got an email that there may be a movie made about me. I mean us. We're even trending on Twitter."

"Seriously, Katherine, I didn't sleep well last night, and I just need to get a nap on the plane."

"Alright then, Hal, I won't talk to you. You just watch, I won't say a word. I wouldn't want to upset you or anything."

Katherine kept her promise until they had finished their onboard lunch of organic chicken breast medallions sautéed with mushrooms in a red wine reduction. "Hal, what are you doing?"

"I'm saving these little salt and pepper shakers. Aren't these the neatest little things? You don't get these back in the cheap seats."

"They're meant to be thrown out with the garbage."

"Really? Well, you didn't use yours at all. Can I have them?"

"Take them then, and be fast because they're picking up the garbage. Oh, I got another email from the college before we left."

"Is April still causing trouble for you?"

"More like causing trouble for herself."

"How's that?"

"You weren't the only one saying someone was in their office, so security kept a watch. They caught her breaking into offices late at night. Somehow she got her hands on a master key and was going through everyone's things."

"Why on earth would she want to do something that stupid?"

"Drugs. That's what they say. They held her for the police, and when the police did a search to see if she stole anything, they found this new designer drug on her."

"You mean that berry drug?"

"Yes. How'd you know what it's called?"

"Long story. I guess she's in jail now."

"You bet she is. And good riddance, if you ask me. She won't be teaching any senior level classes for a long, long time. One more thing, though."

"Yes?"

"What's this I hear about you wanting to replace me as chair?"

"What? Oh, you mean that story in the magazine. Remember, I didn't write that."

"No, I don't mean that at all. You people in my department should know better than gossip. From what I've been told, you've got people ready to have you take over as my replacement. You need to be careful with that sort of talk."

"Katherine, nobody wants to replace you. When your tenure is finished, then people were wondering who should be the next person in charge."

"And you want to do it?"

"No. I guess someone suggested I do it, but I can tell you there's no way I want to. If I had to sit in all the meetings you have to, I'd think I'd jump off the roof."

"Good. Don't you ever get in my way."

They watched the seatback television for an hour although neither could follow the plots of the shows.

"There's something you need to see." Hal retrieved his satchel and removed the small collection of Shakespeare plays. He showed her the names in the back of the book.

"Hal, this is disturbing. You have to turn it in."

"I'm going to. But there's more to it. Remember on that ghost walk when the guide told us about the body of an actor found in the wall?"

"Sure. It was mummified by the peat. Oh, the skeletons in Calgary were found in the wall as well."

"Exactly. I need to check out where this guy travelled to. I bet he left a string of corpses."

"You can do that by yourself. It doesn't sound pleasant at all."

"Excuse me, sir, are you Professor Hal Wales?"

Hal looked up at the stewardess. "Yes."

"Then this would be for you." She handed him a plain white envelope.

"Well open it Hal. Who would send you something in a plane?"

"I really don't want to. I'll look at it later."

"No, this might have something to with me and what I, we, discovered. It might be important."

"Fine then." Hal removed several pages and picked up the top one while Katherine grabbed the others.

"What's that page say, Hal?"

"It's a letter from the Broken Quill Society."

"And they sent it to you? Do they think I work for you or that you're going to be some sort of a lead investigator? When we get home, I'm going to make a phone call and talk to some people about this."

"Karen May sent it."

"Oh, well then, that explains a great deal, doesn't it? So, what does it say, or is it something personal that you don't want me to know about?"

"Have you ever heard of the Agatha Awards? They're given out each year to mystery novelists."

"I can't say I've heard of them."

"They're pretty big in the mystery writing circle. Anyway, there's been a suspicious death at the awards in each of the last three years."

"What do the police say?"

"They don't see a connection, but the society wants us to take a closer look. If we're interested we just need to send an email back to her."

"I'll do that. Sorry, we'll do that when we get home. Does it say anything else?"

"Not really."

"Not really? What does that mean? Tell me what it says."

"Fine then. It says the stewardess she asked to give me the letter is single and I should ask her for a date because she has a nice bottom."

"I am going to call that Ms. May and tell her what I think about sending you a note like that. This isn't junior high, after all."

"What do those pages say?"

"Wait until we get back, Hal. Everything is going to be different between us. You'll need to get in better shape, though, so I'm going to get you a gym membership and make sure you start eating better. And we're going shopping, so you can get some suits and ties and proper black shoes. Hal? Hal, where're you going now?"

"Oh, you can keep talking, Katherine. I think I'm going to say hi to that stewardess. She does have a nice bottom."

ABOUT THE AUTHOR

Kirk Layton lives in Calgary, Canada. From a career in broadcasting, to a career in academics, he has always been fascinated with words.

74686856R00123

Made in the USA
Columbia, SC
07 August 2017